I don't even really know how it happened. I was being way careful, you know? Careful not to fall in love with Jesse, I mean.

And I'd been doing a really good job. I mean, I was getting out and meeting new people and doing new things, just like it says to do in *Cosmo*. I certainly wasn't sitting around mooning over him or anything.

And yeah, okay, the majority of guys I have met since moving to California have turned out either to have psychopathic killers stalking them, or were actually psychopathic killers themselves. But that's really not a very good excuse for falling in love with a ghost. It really isn't.

But that's what happened.

Books by Meg Cabot

THE MEDIATOR 1: SHADOWLAND
THE MEDIATOR 2: NINTH KEY
THE MEDIATOR 3: REUNION
THE MEDIATOR 4: DARKEST HOUR
THE MEDIATOR 5: HAUNTED
THE MEDIATOR 6: TWILIGHT

THE PRINCESS DIARIES
THE PRINCESS DIARIES, VOLUME II: PRINCESS IN THE SPOTLIGHT
THE PRINCESS DIARIES, VOLUME III: PRINCESS IN LOVE
THE PRINCESS DIARIES, VOLUME IV: PRINCESS IN WAITING
THE PRINCESS DIARIES, VOLUME IV AND A HALF: PROJECT PRINCESS
THE PRINCESS DIARIES, VOLUME V: PRINCESS IN PINK
THE PRINCESS DIARIES, VOLUME VI: PRINCESS IN TRAINING
THE PRINCESS PRESENT: A PRINCESS DIARIES BOOK
PRINCESS LESSONS: A PRINCESS DIARIES BOOK
PERFECT PRINCESS: A PRINCESS DIARIES BOOK

ALL-AMERICAN GIRL
TEEN IDOL
NICOLA AND THE VISCOUNT
VICTORIA AND THE ROGUE
THE BOY NEXT DOOR
BOY MEETS GIRL
EVERY BOY'S GOT ONE

THE 1-800-WHERE-R-YOU BOOKS:
WHEN LIGHTNING STRIKES
CODE NAME CASSANDRA
SAFE HOUSE
SANCTUARY

MEG CABOT

the mediator
Darkest Hour

avon books
AN IMPRINT OF HARPERCOLLINS PUBLISHERS

Library of Congress Catalog Card Number: 2004093415
ISBN 0-06-072514-1
First Avon edition, 2005

AVON TRADEMARK REG. U.S. PAT. OFF. AND IN OTHER COUNTRIES,
MARCA REGISTRADA, HECHO EN U.S.A.

❖

11 12 13 OPM 20 19 18 17 16 15 14
Visit us on the World Wide Web!
www.megcabot.com
www.harperteen.com

In memory of
Marcia Mounsey

chapter *one*

Summer. Season of long, slow days and short, hot nights.

Back in Brooklyn, where I spent my first fifteen of them, summer—when it hadn't meant camp—had meant hanging out on the stoop with my best friend, Gina, and her brothers, waiting for the ice-cream truck to come by. When it wasn't too hot, we played a game called War, dividing into teams with the other kids in the neighborhood and shooting each other with imaginary guns.

When we got older, of course, we quit playing War. Gina and I also started laying off the ice cream.

Not that it mattered. None of the neighborhood

guys, the ones we used to play with, wanted anything to do with us. Well, with *me*, anyway. I don't think they'd have minded renewing acquaintances with Gina, but by the time they finally noticed what a babe she'd grown into, she'd set her sights way higher than guys from the 'hood.

I don't know what I expected from my sixteenth summer, my first since moving to California to live with my mom and her new husband . . . and, oh, yeah, his sons. I guess I envisioned the same long, slow days. Only these, in my mind, would be spent at the beach rather than on an apartment building's front stoop.

And as for those short, hot nights, well, I had plans for those, as well. All I needed was a boyfriend.

But as it happened, neither the beach nor the boyfriend materialized, the latter because the guy I liked? Yeah, he so wasn't interested. At least, as far as I could tell. And the former because . . .

Well, because I was forced to get a job.

That's right: A *job*.

I was horrified when one night at dinner, around the beginning of May, my stepfather, Andy, asked me if I'd put in any summer employment applications anywhere. I was all, "What are you *talking* about?"

But it soon became clear that, like the many other sacrifices I'd been asked to make since my mother met, fell in love with, and married Andy Ackerman—host of a popular cable television home improvement program, native Californian, and father of three—my long hot summer lazing at the beach with my friends was not to be.

In the Ackerman household, it soon unfolded, you had two alternatives for how you spent your summer break: a job, or remedial tutoring. Only Doc, my youngest stepbrother—known as David to everyone but me—was exempt from either of these, as he was too young to work, and he had made good enough grades that he'd been accepted into a month-long computer camp, at which he was presumably learning skills that would make him the next Bill Gates—only hopefully without the bad haircut and Wal-Mart-y sweaters.

My second-youngest stepbrother, Dopey (also known as Brad) was not so lucky. Dopey had managed to flunk both English and Spanish—an astounding feat, in my opinion, English being his native language—and so was being forced by his father to attend summer school five days a week . . . when he wasn't being used as unpaid slave labor on the project Andy had undertaken while his TV show was on summer hiatus: tearing down a large portion of our house's backyard deck and installing a hot tub.

Given the alternatives—employment or summer school—I chose to seek employment.

I got a job at the same place my oldest stepbrother, Sleepy, works every summer. He, in fact, recommended me, an act which, at the time, simultaneously stunned and touched me. It wasn't until later that I found out that he had received a small bonus for every person he recommended who was later hired.

Whatever. What it actually boils down to is this: Sleepy—Jake, as he is known to his friends and the rest of the family—and I are now proud employees of the Pebble Beach Hotel and Golf Resort, Sleepy as a lifeguard at one of the resort's many pools, and me as . . .

Well, I signed away my summer to become a hotel staff babysitter.

Okay. You can stop laughing now.

Even I will admit that it's not the kind of job I ever thought I'd be suited for, since I am not long on patience and am certainly not overly fond of having my hair spat up in. But allow me to point out that it does pay ten dollars an hour, and that that does not include tips.

And let me just say that the people who stay at

the Pebble Beach Hotel and Golf Resort? Yeah, they are the kind of people who tend to tip. Generously.

The money, I must say, has gone a long way toward healing my wounded pride. If I have to spend my summer in mindless drudgery, earning a hundred bucks a day—and frequently more—amply compensates for it. Because by the time the summer is over, I should have, without question, the most stunning fall wardrobe of anyone entering the junior class of the Junipero Serra Mission Academy.

So think about *that*, Kelly Prescott, while you spend your summer lounging by your father's pool. I've already got *four* pairs of Jimmy Choos, paid for *with my own money*.

What do you think about that, Little Miss Daddy's AmEx?

The only real problem with my summer job—besides the whiny children and their equally whiny, but loaded, parents, of course—is the fact that I am expected to report there at 8:00 in the morning every day.

That's right. 8:00 A.M. No sleeping in for old Suze this summer.

I must say I find this a bit excessive. And believe me, I've complained. And yet the management staff at the Pebble Beach Hotel and Golf Resort have remained stubbornly unswayed by my persuasive arguments for refraining from offering babysitting services until nine.

And so it is that every morning (I can't even sleep in on Sundays, thanks to my stepfather's insistence that all of us gather around the dining table for the elaborate brunch he prepares; he seems to think we are the Camdens or the Waltons something) I am up before seven. . . .

Which has, I've been surprised to learn, its advantages.

Although I would not list seeing Dopey without a shirt, sweating like a pig, and gulping OJ from the carton as one of them.

There are a lot of girls who go to my school who would, I know, pay money to see Dopey—and Sleepy, too, for that matter—without a shirt, sweat or no sweat. Kelly Prescott, for instance. And her best friend, and Dopey's sometime flame, Debbie Mancuso. I myself do not understand the attraction, but then I can only suppose that these girls have not been around my stepbrothers after a meal in which beans played any sort of role on the menu.

Still, anyone who cared to see Dopey do his calendar pinup imitation could easily do so for free, merely by stopping by our house any week-day morning. For it is in our backyard that Dopey has been, from approximately six in the morning until he has to leave for summer school at ten, stripped to the waist, and performing rigorous manual labor under the eagle eye of his father.

On this particular morning—the one where I caught him, once again, drinking directly from the juice carton, a habit of which my mother and I have been trying, with little success, to cure the entire Ackerman clan—Dopey had apparently been doing some digging, since he left a trail of mud along the kitchen floor, in addition to a dirt-encrusted object on what had once been an immaculate counter (I should know: It had been my turn to 409 it the night before).

"Oh," I said, as I stepped into the kitchen. "Isn't that a lovely picture."

Dopey lowered the orange juice container and looked at me.

"Don't you have somewhere to be?" he asked, wiping his mouth with the back of a wrist.

"Of course," I said. "But I was hoping that before I left, I could enjoy a nice glass of calcium-fortified juice. I see now that that will not be possible."

Dopey shook the carton. "There's still some left," he said.

"Mixed with your backwash?" I heaved a shudder. "I think not."

Dopey opened his mouth to say something—presumably his usual suggestion that I chew on some piece of his anatomy—but his father's voice called from outside the sliding glass doors to the deck.

"Brad," Andy yelled. "That's enough of a break. Get back out here and help me lower this."

Dopey slammed down the carton of OJ. Before he could stalk from the room, however, I stopped him with a polite, "Excuse me?"

Because he wore no shirt, I could see the muscles in Dopey's neck and shoulders tense as I spoke.

"All right already," he said, spinning around and heading back toward the juice carton. "I'll put it away. Jeez, why are you always *on* me about crap like—"

"I don't care about *that*," I interrupted him, pointing at the juice carton—although it had to have been making the counter sticky. "I want to know what *that* is."

Dopey looked where I'd moved my finger. He blinked down at the dirt-encrusted oblong object.

"I dunno," he said. "I found it buried in the yard while I was digging out one of the posts."

I gingerly lifted what appeared to be a metal box, about six inches long by two inches thick, heavily rusted and covered in mud. There were a few places where the mud had rubbed off, though, and there you could see some words painted on the box. The few I could make out were *delicious aroma* and *quality assured*. When I shook the box, it rattled. There was something inside.

"What's in it?" I asked Dopey.

He shrugged. "How should I know? It's rusted shut. I was gonna take a—"

I never did find out what Dopey was going to do to the box, since his older brother, Sleepy, walked into the kitchen at that moment, reached for the orange juice carton, opened it, and downed the remaining contents. When he was through, he crumpled the carton, threw it into the trash compactor, and then, apparently noticing my appalled expression, said, *"What?"*

I don't get what girls see in them. Seriously. They are like *animals*.

And not the cute fuzzy kind, either.

Meanwhile, outside, Andy was calling imperiously for Dopey again.

Dopey muttered some extremely colorful four-letter words beneath his breath, then shouted, "I'm *coming*, already," and stomped outside.

It was already 7:45, so Sleepy and I really had to "motor," as he put it, to get to the resort on time. But though my eldest stepbrother has a tendency to sleepwalk through life, there's nothing somnambulistic about his driving. I punched in at work with five minutes to spare.

The Pebble Beach Hotel and Golf Resort prides itself on its efficiency. And it is, in fact, a very smoothly run operation. As a staff babysitter, it's my responsibility, after punching in, to ask for my assignment for the day. That's when I find out whether I'll be washing strained carrots or burger fixings out of my hair after work. On the whole, I prefer burgers, but there's something to be said for strained carrots: generally the people who eat them can't talk back to you.

When I heard my assignment for that particular day, however, I was disappointed, even though it was a burger-eater.

"Simon, Susannah," Caitlin called. "You're assigned to Slater, Jack."

"For God's sake," I said to Caitlin, who was my supervisor. "I was stuck with Jack Slater yesterday. *And* the day before."

Caitlin is only two years older than me, but she treats me like I'm twelve. In fact, I'm sure the only reason she tolerates me is because of Sleepy:

10

She is as warm for his form as every other girl on this planet . . . except, of course, me.

"Jack's parents," Caitlin informed me, without even looking up from her clipboard, "requested you, Suze."

"Couldn't you have said I was already taken?"

Caitlin did look up then. She looked at me with cool, blue contact-lensed eyes. "Suze," she said. "They *like* you."

I fiddled with my bathing suit straps. I was wearing the regulation navy blue swimsuit beneath my regulation navy blue Oxford T-shirt and khaki shorts. With *pleats*, no less. Appalling.

I mentioned the uniform, right? I mean, the part where I have to wear a uniform to work? No kidding. Every day. A uniform.

If I'd known about the uniform beforehand, I never would have applied for the job.

"Yeah," I said. "I know they like me."

The feeling isn't mutual. It isn't that I don't like Jack, although he's easily the whiniest little kid I have ever met. I mean, you can see why he's that way—just take a look at his parents, a pair of career-obsessed physicians who think dumping their kid off with a hotel babysitter for days on end while they go sailing and golfing is a fine family vacation.

It's actually Jack's older brother I have the problem with. Well, not necessarily a *problem* . . .

More like I would just rather avoid seeing him while I am wearing my incredibly unstylish Pebble Beach Hotel and Golf Resort uniform khaki shorts.

Yeah. The ones with the pleats in them.

Except, of course, that every time I've run into the guy since he and his family arrived at the resort last week, I've been wearing the stupid things.

Not that I care, particularly, what Paul Slater thinks about me. I mean, my heart, to coin a phrase, belongs to another.

Too bad he shows no signs whatsoever of actually wanting it. My heart, that is.

Still, Paul—that's his name; Jack's older brother, I mean: Paul Slater—is pretty incredible. I mean, it isn't just that he's a hottie. Oh, no. Paul's hot *and* funny. Every time I go to pick Jack up or drop him off at his family's hotel suite, and his brother, Paul, happens to be there, he always has some flippant remark to make about the hotel or his parents or himself. Not mean or anything. Just funny.

And I think he's smart, too, because whenever he isn't on the golf course with his dad or playing tennis with his mom, he's at the pool reading. And not your typical pool book, either. No Clancy or Crichton or King for Paul. Oh, no. We're talking stuff by guys like Nietzsche, or Kierkegaard.

Seriously. It's almost enough to make you think he's not from California.

And of course it turns out, he's not: The Slaters are visiting from Seattle.

So you see, it wasn't just that Jack Slater is the whiniest kid I've ever met: There was also the fact that I wasn't really all that enthused about his hottie brother seeing me, yet again, in shorts that make my butt look roughly the size of Montana.

But Caitlin was totally uninterested in my personal feelings on the matter.

"Suze," Caitlin said, looking down at her clipboard again. "Nobody likes Jack. But the fact is, Dr. and Mrs. Slater like you. So you're spending the day with Jack. Capisce?"

I sighed gustily, but what could I do? Aside from my pride, my tan was the only thing that was really going to suffer from spending yet another day with Jack. The kid doesn't like swimming, or bike riding, or Rollerblading, or Frisbee tossing, or anything, really, to do with the great outdoors. His idea of a good time is to sit inside the hotel room and watch cartoons.

I'm not kidding, either. He is, without a doubt, the most boring kid I ever met. I find it hard to believe he and Paul came from the same gene pool.

"Besides," Caitlin added, as I was standing there, fuming. "Today is Jack's eighth birthday."

I stared at her. "His *birthday*? It's Jack's *birthday*, and his parents are leaving him with a sitter all day?"

Caitlin shot me a severe look. "The Slaters say they'll be back in time to take him to dinner at the Grill."

The Grill. Whoopee. The Grill is the fanciest restaurant at the resort, maybe even on the entire peninsula. The cheapest thing they serve there costs about fifteen dollars, and that's the house salad. The Grill is so *not* a fun place to take a kid on his eighth birthday. I mean, even Jack, the most boring child in the world, couldn't have a fun time there.

I don't get it. I really don't. I mean, what's wrong with these people? And how, seeing the way they treat their youngest child, had their other one managed to turn out so . . .

Well, *hot*?

At least, that was the word that flashed through my mind as Paul opened the door to his family's suite in response to my knock, then stood there grinning down at me, one hand in the pocket of his cream-colored chinos, the other clutching a book by someone called Martin Heidegger.

Yeah, you know what the last book I read was? That'd be *Clifford*. That's right. The big red dog. And okay, I was reading it to a five-year-old, but still. Heidegger. Jeez.

"All right. Who called Room Service and ordered the pretty girl?" Paul wanted to know.

Well, okay, that wasn't funny. That was actually sort of sexually harassing, if you think about it. But the fact that the guy saying it was my age, about six feet tall, and olive-complected, with curly brown hair and eyes as blue as the ocean just beyond the Pebble Beach golf course, made it not so bad.

Not so bad. What am I talking about? The guy could sexually harass me anytime he wanted to. At least *someone* wanted to.

Just my luck it wasn't the guy I wanted.

I didn't admit this out loud, of course. What I said instead was, "Ha ha. I'm here for Jack."

Paul winced. "Oh," he said, shaking his head in mock disappointment. "The little guy gets all the luck."

He held the door open for me, and I stepped

into the suite's plush living room. Jack was where he usually was, sprawled on the floor in front of the TV. He did not acknowledge my presence, as was his custom.

His mother, on the other hand, did acknowledge me: "Oh, hi, Susan. Rick and Paul and I will be on the course all morning. And then the three of us are meeting for lunch at the Grotto, and then we've got appointments with our personal trainers. So if you could stay until we all get back, around seven, we'd appreciate it. Make sure Jack has a bath before changing for dinner. I've laid out a suit for him. It's his birthday, you know. Okay, buh-bye, you two. Have fun, Jack."

"How could he not?" Paul wanted to know, with a meaningful glance in my direction.

And then the Slaters left.

Jack remained where he was—in front of the TV, not speaking to me, not even looking at me. As this was typical Jack behavior, I was not alarmed.

I crossed the room—stepping over Jack on my way—and went to fling open the wide French doors that led out onto a terrace overlooking the sea. Rick and Nancy Slater were paying six hundred dollars a night for their view, which was one of the Monterey Bay, sparkling turquoise under a cloudless blue sky. From their suite you could see the yellow slice of beach upon which, were it not for my well-meaning but misguided stepfather, I would have been whiling away my summer.

It isn't fair. It really isn't.

"Okay, big guy," I said, after taking in the view for a minute or two and listening to the soothing pulse of the waves. "Go put on your swim trunks. We're hitting the pool. It's too nice out to stay inside."

Jack, as usual, looked as if I'd pinched him rather than suggested a fun day at the pool.

"But *why*?" he cried. "You know I can't swim."

"Which is exactly," I said, "why we're going. You're eight years old today. An eight-year-old who can't swim is nothing but a loser. You don't want to be a loser, do you?"

Jack opined that he preferred being a loser to going outdoors, a fact with which I was only too well acquainted.

"Jack," I said, slumping down onto a couch near where he lay. "What is your problem?"

Instead of responding, Jack rolled over onto his stomach and scowled at the carpet. I wasn't going to let up on him, though. I knew what I was talking about, with the loser thing. Being different in the American public—or even private—educational system is not cool. How Paul had ever allowed this to happen—his little brother's turning into a whiny little wimp you almost longed to slap—I couldn't fathom, but I knew good and well Rick and Nancy weren't doing anything to help rectify the matter. It was pretty much all up to me to save Jack Slater from becoming his school's human punching bag.

Don't ask me why I even cared. Maybe because in a weird way, Jack reminded me a little of Doc, my youngest stepbrother, the one who is away at computer camp. A geek in the truest sense of the word, Doc is still one of my favorite people. I have even been making a concerted effort to call him by his name, David . . . at least to his face.

But Doc is—almost—able to get away with his bizarre behavior because he has a photographic memory and a computerlike ability to process information. Jack, so far as I could tell, possessed no such skills. In fact, I had a feeling he was a bit dim. So really, he had no excuse for his eccentricities.

"What's the deal?" I asked him. "Don't you *want* to learn how to swim and throw a Frisbee, like a normal person?"

"You don't understand," Jack said, not very distinctly, into the carpet. "I'm *not* a normal person. I—I'm different than other people."

"Of course you are," I said, rolling my eyes. "We're all special and unique, like snowflakes. But there's different, and then there's freakish. And you, Jack, are going to turn freakish, if you don't watch out."

"I—I already am freakish," Jack said.

But he wouldn't elaborate, and I can't say I pressed too hard, trying to find out what he meant. Not that I imagined he might like to drown kittens in his spare time, or anything like that. I just figured he meant freakish in the general sense. I mean, we all feel like freaks from time to time. Jack maybe felt like one a bit more often than that, but then, with Rick and Nancy for parents, who wouldn't? He was probably constantly being asked why he couldn't be more like his older brother, Paul. That would be enough to make any kid feel a little insecure. I mean, come on. *Heidegger*? On summer *vacation*?

Give me *Clifford* any day.

I told Jack that worrying so much was going to make him old before his time. Then I ordered him to go and put on his swimsuit.

He did so, but he didn't exactly hurry, and when we finally got outside and onto the brick path to the pool, it was almost 10:00. The sun was beating down hard, though it wasn't uncomfortably hot yet. Actually, it hardly ever gets uncomfortably hot in Carmel, even in the middle of July. Back in Brooklyn, you can barely go outdoors in July, it's so muggy. In Carmel, however, there is next to no humidity, and there's always a cool breeze from the Pacific. . . .

Perfect date weather, actually. If you happened to have one. A date, I mean. Which, of course, I don't. And probably never will—at least with the guy I want—if things keep up the way they've been going.

Anyway, Jack and I were tripping down the brick path to the pool when one of the gardeners stepped out from behind an enormous forsythia bush and nodded to me.

This wouldn't have been at all odd—I have actually gotten friendly with all of the landscaping staff, thanks to the many Frisbees I have lost while playing with my charges—except for the fact that this particular gardener, Jorge, who had been expected to retire at the end of the summer, had instead suffered a heart attack a few days earlier, and, well . . .

Died.

Yet there was Jorge in his beige coveralls, holding a pair of hedge clippers and bobbing his head at me, just as he had the last time I'd seen him, on this very path, a few days before.

I wasn't too worried about Jack's reaction to having a dead man walk up and nod at us, since for the most part, I'm the only one I know who can actually see them. The dead, I mean. So I was perfectly unprepared for what happened next. . . .

Which was that Jack ripped his hand from mine and, with a strangled scream, ran for the pool.

This was odd, but then, so was Jack. I rolled my eyes at Jorge, then hurried after the kid, since I am, after all, getting paid to care for the living. The whole helping-out-the-dead thing has to play second fiddle so long as I'm on the Pebble Beach Hotel and Golf Resort time clock. The ghosts simply have to wait. I mean, it's not as if they're paying me. Ha! I wish.

I found Jack huddled on a deck chair, sobbing into his towel. Fortunately, it was still early enough that there weren't many people at the pool yet. Otherwise, I might have had some explaining to do.

But the only other person there was Sleepy, high up in his lifeguard chair. And it was pretty clear from the way Sleepy was resting his cheek in one hand that his shutters, behind the lenses of his Ray-Bans, were closed.

"Jack," I said, sinking down onto the neighboring deck chair. "Jack, what's the matter?"

"I . . . I t-told you already," Jack sobbed into his fluffy white towel. "Suze . . . I'm not *like* other people. I'm like what you said. A . . . a . . . freak."

I didn't know what he was talking about. I assumed he was merely continuing our conversation from the room.

"Jack," I said. "You're no more a freak than anybody else."

"No," he sobbed. "I *am*. Don't you get it?" Then he lifted his head, looked me straight in the eye, and hissed, "Suze, don't you know why I don't like to go outside?"

I shook my head. I didn't get it. Even then, I still didn't get it.

"Because when I go outside," Jack whispered, "*I see dead people*."

chap*two*ter

I swear that's what he said.

He said it just like the kid in that movie said it, too, with the same tears in his eyes, the same fear in his voice.

And I had much the same reaction as I had when watching the movie. I went, inwardly, *Freaking crybaby*.

Outwardly, however, I said only, "So?"

I didn't mean to sound callous. Really. I was just so surprised. I mean, in all my sixteen years, I've only met one other person with the same ability I have—the ability to see and speak with the dead—and that person is a sixty-something-year-old priest who also happens to be principal of the school I am currently attending. I certainly never expected to meet up with a fellow mediator at the Pebble Beach Hotel and Golf Resort.

But Jack took offense at my "So?" anyway.

"*So?*" Jack sat up. He was a skinny little kid, with a caved-in sort of chest, and curly brown hair like his brother's. Only Jack lacked his brother's nicely buff shape, so the curly hair, which looked sublime on Paul, gave Jack the unfortunate appearance of a walking Q-tip.

I don't know. Maybe that's why Rick and Nancy don't want to hang around him. Jack's a little creepy looking, and apparently has frequent dialogues with the dead. God knows it never made me Miss Popularity.

The talking to the dead thing, I mean. I am not creepy looking. In fact, when I am not wearing my uniform shorts, I am frequently complimented on my appearance by the occasional construction worker.

"Didn't you hear what I said?" Jack was depressed, you could tell. I was probably the first person he'd ever told about his unique problem who'd been completely unimpressed.

Poor kid. He had no idea who he was dealing with.

"I see dead people," he said, rubbing his eyes

with his fists. "They come up and start talking to me. And they're *dead.*"

I leaned forward, resting my elbows on my knees.

"Jack," I said.

"You don't believe me." His chin started trembling. "No one believes me. But it's true!"

Jack buried his face in his towel again. I glanced in Sleepy's direction. Still no sign that he was aware of either of us, much less that he found Jack's behavior at all odd. The kid was murmuring about all the people who hadn't believed him over the years, a list that seemed to include not only his parents, but a whole stream of medical specialists Rick and Nancy had dragged him to, hoping to cure their youngest child of this delusion he has—that he can speak to the dead.

Poor little guy. He hadn't realized, as I had from a very early age, that what he and I can do . . . well, you just don't talk about it.

I sighed. Really, it would have been too much to ask, apparently, for me to have a *normal* summer. I mean, a summer without any paranormal incidents.

But then, I'd never had one of those before in my life. Why should my sixteenth summer be any different?

I reached out and laid a hand on one of Jack's thin, quivering shoulders.

"Jack," I said. "You saw that gardener just now, didn't you? The one with the hedge clippers?"

Jack lifted an astonished, tear-stained face from the terry cloth. He stared up at me in wonder.

"You . . . you saw him, too?"

"Yeah," I said. "That was Jorge. He used to work here. He died a couple days ago of a heart attack."

"But how could you—" Jack shook his head slowly back and forth. "I mean, he's . . . he's a ghost."

"Well, yeah," I said. "He probably has something he needs us to do for him. He kicked off kind of suddenly, and there may be stuff, you know, he left unfinished. He came up to us because he wants our help."

"That's . . . " Jack stared at me. "That's why they come up to me? Because they want help?"

"Well, yeah," I said. "What else would they want?"

"I don't know." Jack's lower lip started to tremble again. "To kill me."

I couldn't help smiling a little at that one. "No, Jack," I said. "That's not why ghosts come up to you. Not because they want to kill you." Not yet, anyway. The kid was too young to have made the kind of homicidal enemies I had. "They come up to you because you're a mediator, like me."

Tears trembled on the edges of Jack's long eyelashes as he gazed up at me. "A . . . a what?"

Oh, for God's sake, I thought. *Why me?* I mean, really. Like my life's not complicated enough. Now I have to play Obi Wan Kenobi to this kid's Anakin Skywalker? It so isn't fair. When was I ever going to get the chance to be a normal teenage girl, to do the things normal teenage girls like to do, like go to parties and hang out at the beach, and, um, what else?

Oh, yeah, date. A date, with the boy I actually like, would be nice.

But do I get dates? Oh, no. What do I get instead?

Ghosts. Mainly ghosts looking for help cleaning up the messes they made when they were alive, but sometimes ghosts whose sole amusement appears to be making even bigger messes in the lives of the people they left behind. And this frequently includes mine.

I ask you, do I have a big sign on my forehead that says Maid Service? Why am I always the one who has to tidy up other people's messes?

Because I had the misfortune to be born a mediator.

I must say, I think I'm way better suited for the job than poor Jack. I mean, I saw my first ghost when I was two years old, and I can assure you, my initial reaction was not fear. Not that, at the age of two, I'd been able to help the poor suffering soul who approached me. But I hadn't shrieked and run away in terror, either.

It wasn't until later, after my dad—who passed away when I was six—came back and explained it that I began to fully understand what I was, and why I could see the dead, but others—like my mom, for instance—could not.

One thing I did know, though, from a very tender age: mentioning to anyone that I could see folks they couldn't? Yeah, not such a hot idea. Not if I didn't want to end up on the ninth floor of Bellevue, which is where they stick all the whackos in New York City.

Only Jack didn't seem to have quite the same instinctive sense of self-preservation I'd apparently been born with. He'd been opening up his trap about the whole ghost thing to anyone who would listen, with the inevitable result that his poor parents didn't want to have anything to do with him. I'd be willing to bet that kids his own age, figuring he was lying to get attention, felt the same way. In a sense, the little guy had brought all his current misfortunes down upon himself.

On the other hand, if you ask me, whoever is up there handing out the mediator badges needs to make a better effort to see that the folks who get awarded the job are mentally up to the challenge. I complain a lot about it because it has put a significant cramp in my social life, but there is nothing about this whole mediator thing I do not feel perfectly capable of handling. . . .

Well, except for one thing.

But I've been making a concerted effort not to think about that.

Or rather, *him*.

"A mediator," I explained to Jack, "is someone who helps people who have died to move on, into their next life." Or wherever people go when they kick the bucket. But I didn't want to get into a whole metaphysical discussion with this kid. I mean, he is, after all, only eight.

"You mean like I'm supposed to help them go to heaven?" Jack asked.

"Well, yeah, I guess." If there is one.

"But . . . " Jack shook his head. "I don't know anything about heaven."

"You don't have to." I tried to think how to explain it to him, then decided showing was better than telling. That's what Mr. Walden, who I had last year for English and world civ, was always saying, anyway.

"Look," I said, taking Jack by the hand. "Come on. Watch me, and you can see how it works."

Jack put the brakes on right away, though.

"No," he gasped, his blue eyes, so like his brother's, wild with fear. "No, I don't want to."

I yanked him to his feet. Hey, I never said I was cut out for this babysitting thing, remember?

"Come on," I said again. "Jorge won't hurt you. He's really nice. Let's see what he wants."

I practically had to carry him, but I finally got Jack over to where we'd last seen Jorge. A moment later the gardener—or, I should say, his spirit—reappeared, and after a lot of polite nodding and smiling, we got down to business. It was kind of hard, considering that Jorge's English was about as good as my Spanish—which is to say, not good at all—but eventually, I was able to figure out what was keeping Jorge from moving on from this life to his next—whatever that might be: His sister had appropriated a rosary left by their mother for her first grandchild, Jorge's daughter.

"So," I explained to Jack, as I steered him into the hotel lobby, "what we have to do is get Jorge's sister to give the rosary back to Teresa, his daughter.

Otherwise, Jorge will just keep hanging around and pestering us. Oh, and he won't be able to find eternal rest. Got it?"

Jack said nothing. He just wandered behind me in a daze. He had been silent as death during my conversation with Jorge, and now he looked as if someone had whacked him on the back of the head with a Wiffle bat a couple hundred times.

"Come here," I said, and steered Jack into a fancy mahogany phone booth with a sliding glass door. After we'd both slipped through it, I pulled the door shut, then picked up the phone and fed a quarter into the slot. "Watch and learn, grasshopper," I said to him.

What followed was a fairly typical example of what I do on an almost daily basis. I called information, got the guilty party's phone number, then phoned her. When she picked up, and I ascertained that she spoke enough English to understand me, I informed her of the facts as I knew them, without the least embellishment. When you are dealing with the undead, there's no need for exaggeration of any kind. The fact that someone who has died has contacted you with details no one but the deceased could know is generally enough. By the end of our conversation, an obviously flustered Marisol had assured me that the rosary would be delivered, that day, into Teresa's hands.

End of conversation. I thanked Jorge's sister and hung up.

"Now," I explained to Jack, "if Marisol doesn't do it, we'll hear from Jorge again, and we'll have to resort to something a little more persuasive than a mere phone call. But she sounded pretty scared. It's spooky when a perfect stranger calls you and tells you she's spoken to your dead brother, and that he's mad at you. I bet she'll do it."

Jack stared up at me. "That's it?" he asked. "That's all he wanted you to do? Get his sister to give the necklace back?"

"Rosary," I corrected him. "And yes, that was it."

I didn't think it was important to add that this had been a particularly simple case. Usually, the problems associated with people speaking from beyond the grave are a little more complicated and take a lot more than a simple phone call to settle. In fact, oftentimes, fisticuffs are involved. I had only just recently recovered from a few broken ribs given to me by a group of ghosts who hadn't appreciated my attempts to help them into the afterlife one little bit, and had, in fact, ended up putting me in the hospital.

But Jack had plenty of time to learn that not all the undead were like Jorge. Besides, it was his birthday. I didn't want to bum him out.

So instead, I slid the phone booth door open again and said, "Let's go swimming."

Jack was so stunned by the whole thing he didn't even protest. He still had questions, of course . . . questions I answered as patiently and thoroughly as I could. In between questions, I taught him to freestyle.

And I don't want to brag or anything, but I have to say that, thanks to my careful instructions and calming influence, by the end of the day Jack Slater was acting like—and even swimming like—a normal eight-year-old.

I'm not kidding. The little dude had completely lightened up. He was even *laughing*. It was as if showing him that he had nothing to fear from the ghosts who had been plaguing him his whole life had lifted from him his fear of . . . well, everything. It wasn't long before he was running around the pool deck, doing cannonballs off the side, and annoying all the doctors' wives who were trying to tan themselves in the nearby lounge chairs. Just like any other eight-year-old boy.

He even struck up a conversation with a group

of other kids who were being tended by one of my fellow sitters. And when one of them splashed water in Jack's face, instead of bursting into tears, as he would have done the day before, Jack splashed the kid back, causing Kim, my fellow sitter, who was treading water beside me, to ask, "My God, Suze, what did you do to Jack Slater? He's acting almost . . . *normal*."

I tried not to let my pride show.

"Oh, you know," I said with a shrug. "I just taught him to swim, is all. I guess that gave him some confidence."

Kim watched as Jack and another boy, just to be irritating, did double cannonballs into a group of little girls, who shrieked and then tried to hit the boys with their foam floaties.

"God," Kim said. "I'll say. I can't believe it's even the same kid."

Neither, it became apparent, could Jack's own family. I was teaching him the backstroke when I heard someone whistle, low and long, from the far side of the pool. Jack and I both looked up and saw Paul standing there, looking all Pete Sampras-y in white and holding a tennis racquet.

"Well, would you look at that," Paul drawled. "My brother, in a pool. And enjoying himself, no less. Has hell frozen over, or something?"

"Paul," Jack screamed. "Watch me! Watch me!"

And the next thing any of us knew, Jack was racing through the water toward his brother. I wouldn't exactly call what Jack was doing a proper crawl, but it was a close enough imitation of it to pass, even in an older brother's eyes. And if it wasn't pretty, there was no denying the kid was staying afloat. You had to give him that.

And Paul did. He squatted down and, when Jack's head bobbed up just beneath him, he reached down and pushed it under again. You know, in a playful way.

"Congrats, champ," Paul said when Jack resurfaced. "I never thought I'd live to see the day you wouldn't be afraid to get your face wet."

Jack, beaming, said, "Watch me swim back!" and began to thrash through the water to the other side of the pool. Again, not pretty, but effective.

But Paul, instead of watching his brother swim, looked down at me, standing chest-high in the clear blue water.

"All right, Annie Sullivan," he said. "What have you done to Helen?"

I shrugged. Jack had never mentioned his brother's feelings on the whole I-see-dead-people thing, so I didn't know if Paul was aware of Jack's ability or if he, like his parents, thought it was all in the kid's head. One of the points I'd tried to impress upon Jack was that the fewer people—particularly adults—who knew, the better. I had forgotten to ask if Paul knew.

Or, more important, believed.

"Just taught him how to swim is all," I said, sweeping some of my wet hair from my face.

I won't lie or anything and say I was embarrassed for a hottie like Paul to see me in my swimsuit. I look a lot better in the navy blue one-piece suit the hotel forces us to wear than I do in those heinous shorts.

Plus my mascara is totally the waterproof kind. I mean, I'm not an idiot.

"My parents have been trying to get that kid to swim for six years," Paul said. "And you do it in one day?"

I smiled at him. "I'm extremely persuasive," I said.

Yeah, okay, I was flirting. So sue me. A girl has to have *some* fun.

"You," Paul said, "are nothing short of a miracle worker. Come have dinner with us tonight."

All of a sudden, I didn't feel like flirting anymore.

"Oh, no, thank you," I said.

"Come on," Paul said. I have to say that he looked exceptionally fine in his white shirt and shorts. They brought out the deepness of his tan, just like the late afternoon sunlight brought out the occasional strand of gold in his otherwise dark brown curls.

And a tan wasn't all Paul had that the other hottie in my life didn't: Paul also happened to have a heartbeat.

"Why not?" Paul was kneeling by the side of pool, one dark forearm resting across an equally dark knee. "My parents will be delighted. And it's clear my brother can't live without you. And we're going to the Grill. You can't turn down an invitation to the Grill."

"I'm sorry," I said. "I really can't. Hotel policy. The staff aren't supposed to mingle with the guests."

"Who said anything about mingling?" Paul wanted to know. "I'm talking about eating. Come on. Give the kid a birthday treat."

"I really can't," I said, flashing him my best smile. "I have to go. Sorry."

And I swam over to where Jack was struggling to lift himself onto a huge pile of floaties he'd collected, and pretended to be too busy helping him to hear Paul calling to me.

Look, I know what you're thinking. You're thinking I said no because the whole thing would just be too *Dirty Dancing*, right? Summer fling at the resort, only with the roles reversed: you know, the poor working girl and the rich doctor's son, nobody puts Baby in the corner, blah blah blah. That kind of thing.

But that's not it. Not really. For one thing, I'm not even technically poor. I mean, I'm making ten bucks an hour here, plus tips. And my mom is a TV news anchorwoman, and my stepdad has his own show, too.

And okay, sure, it's only local news, and Andy's show is on cable, but come on. We have a house in the Carmel Hills.

And okay, yeah, the house is a converted hundred-and-fifty-year-old hotel. But we each have our own bedroom, and there are three cars parked in the driveway, none of which are propped up on cinderblocks. We don't exactly qualify for food stamps.

And it isn't even that other thing I mentioned, about there being a policy against staff mingling with the guests. There isn't any such policy.

As Kim felt obligated to point out to me a few minutes later.

"What is your glitch, Simon?" she wanted to know. "That guy's got the hots for you, and you went completely Red Baron on him. I never saw anybody get shot down so fast."

I busied myself scooping a drowning ant off the surface of the water. "I'm, um, busy tonight," I said.

"Don't give me that, Suze." Although I had never met Kim before we'd started working together—she goes to Carmel Valley High, the public school my mother is convinced is riddled with drug addicts and gangbangers—we'd gotten pretty close due to our mutual dissatisfaction at being forced to rise so early in the morning for work. "You aren't doing anything tonight. So what's with the antiaircraft fire?"

I finally captured the ant. Keeping it cupped in my palm, I made my way toward the side of the pool.

"I don't know," I said as I waded. "He seems nice and all. The thing is"—I shook my hand out over the side of the pool, setting the ant free—"I kind of like somebody else."

Kim raised her eyebrows. One of them had a little hole in it where she normally wears a gold stud. Caitlin makes her take it out before work, though.

"Tell," Kim commanded.

I glanced involuntarily up at Sleepy, dozing in his lifeguard's chair. Kim let out a little shriek.

"Eew," she cried. "*Him?* But he's your—"

I rolled my eyes. "No, not *him*. God. Just . . . Look, I just like somebody else, okay? But it's like . . . it's a secret."

Kim sucked in her breath. "Ooh," she said. "The best kind. Does he go to the Academy?" When I shook my head, she tried, "Robert Louis Stevenson School, then?"

Again, I shook my head.

Kim wrinkled up her nose. "He doesn't go to CVHS, does he?"

I sighed. "He isn't in high school, okay, Kim? I'd really rather—"

"Oh my God," Kim said. "A *college* guy? You dog. My mom would *kill* me if she knew I was going with a college guy—"

"He's not in college, either, okay?" I could feel my cheeks growing warm. "Look, the thing is, it's complicated. And I don't want to talk about it."

Kim looked taken aback. "Well, all right. God. Sorry."

But she couldn't leave well enough alone.

"He's older, right?" she asked, less than a minute later. "Like *way* older? That's okay, you know. I went out with an older guy, like, when I was fourteen. He was eighteen. My mom didn't know. So I can totally relate."

"Somehow," I said, "I really don't think you can."

She wrinkled her nose again. "God," she said. "How old is he?"

I thought about telling her. I thought about going, *Oh, I don't know. About a century and a half.*

But I didn't. Instead I told Jack it was time to go inside, if he was going to have a bath before dinner.

"Jeez," I heard Kim say as I got out. "*That* old, huh?"

Yeah. Unfortunately. *That* old.

chapter *three*

I don't even really know how it happened. I was being way careful, you know? Careful not to fall in love with Jesse, I mean.

And I'd been doing a really good job. I mean, I was getting out and meeting new people and doing new things, just like it says to do in *Cosmo*. I certainly wasn't sitting around mooning over him or anything.

And yeah, okay, the majority of guys I have met since moving to California have turned out either to have psychopathic killers stalking them, or were actually psychopathic killers themselves. But that's really not a very good excuse for falling in love with a ghost. It really isn't.

But that's what happened.

I can tell you the exact moment I knew it was all over, too. My battle to keep from falling in love with him, I mean. It was while I was in the hospital, recovering from that severe butt-kicking I mentioned before—the one I got courtesy of the ghosts of four RLS students who had been murdered a few weeks before school let out for the summer.

Anyway, Jesse showed up in my hospital room (Why not? He's a ghost. He can materialize anywhere he wants.) to express his get-well wishes, which were extremely heartfelt and all, and while he was there, he happened, at one point, to reach out and touch my cheek.

That's all. He just touched my cheek, which was, I believe, the only part of me that was not black and blue at the time.

Big deal, right? So he touched my cheek. That's no reason to swoon.

But I did.

Oh, not literally. It wasn't like anybody had to wave smelling salts under my nose or anything, for God's sake. But after that, I was gone. Done for. Toast.

I flatter myself I've done a pretty good job of hiding it. He, I'm sure, has no idea. I still treat him as if he were . . . well, an ant that has fallen into my pool. You know, irritating, but not worth killing.

And I haven't told anyone. How can I? No one—except for Father Dominic, back at the Academy, and my youngest stepbrother, Doc—has any idea Jesse even exists. I mean, come on, the ghost of a guy who died a hundred and fifty years ago, and lives in my bedroom? If I mentioned it to anyone, they'd cart me off to the loony bin faster than you can say *Stir of Echoes*.

But it's there. Just because I haven't told anyone doesn't mean it isn't there, all the time, lurking in the back of my mind, like one of those 'NSync songs you can't get out of your head.

And I have to tell you, it makes the idea of going out with other guys seem like . . . well, a big waste of time.

So I didn't jump at the chance to go out with Paul Slater (though if you ask me, having dinner with him *and* his parents *and* his little brother hardly qualifies as going out). Instead, I went home and had dinner with my own parents and brothers. Well, stepbrothers, anyway.

Dinner in the Ackerman household was always this very big deal . . . until Andy started working on installing the hot tub. Since then, he has slacked off considerably in the culinary department, let me tell you. And since my mom is hardly what you'd call a cook, we've been enjoying a lot of takeout lately. I thought we had hit rock bottom the night before, when we'd actually ordered from Peninsula Pizza, the place Sleepy works nights as a delivery guy.

But I didn't know how bad it could get until I walked in that night and saw a red-and-white bucket sitting in the middle of the table.

"Don't start," my mother said when she noticed me.

I just shook my head. "I guess if you peel the skin off, it's not that bad for you."

"Give it to me," Dopey said, glopping semi-congealed mashed potatoes onto his plate. "I'll eat your skin."

I could hardly control my gag reflex after that offer, but I managed, and I was reading the nutritional literature that came with our meal—"The Colonel has never forgotten the delicious aromas that used to float from his mother's kitchen on the plantation back when he was a boy"—when I remembered the tin box, the contents of which had also been advertised as having a delicious aroma.

"Hey," I said. "So what was in that box you guys dug up?"

Dopey made a face. "Nothing. Bunch of old letters."

Andy looked sadly at his son. The truth is, I think even my stepfather has begun to realize what I have known since the day I met him: that his middle son is a bohunk.

"Not just a bunch of old letters, Brad," Andy said. "They're quite old, dated around the time this house was built—1850. They're in extremely poor condition—falling apart, actually. I was thinking of taking them over to the historical society. They might want them, in spite of the condition. Or"—Andy looked at me—"I thought Father Dominic might be interested. You know what a history buff he is."

Father Dom is a history buff, all right, but only because, like me, as a mediator he has a tendency to run into people who have actually lived through historical events like the Alamo and the Lewis and Clark expedition. You know, folks who take the phrase *Been there, done that* to a whole new level.

"I'll give him a call," I said as I accidentally dropped a piece of chicken into my lap, where it was immediately vacuumed up by the Ackermans' enormous dog, Max, who maintains a watchful position at my side during every meal.

It was only when Dopey chortled that I realized I'd said the wrong thing. Never having been a normal teenage girl, it is sometimes hard for me to imitate one. And normal teenage girls do not, I know, give their high school principals calls on any sort of regular basis.

I glared at Dopey from across the table.

"I was going to call him anyway," I said, "to find out what I'm supposed to do with the left-over cash from our class trip to Six Flags."

"I'll take it," Sleepy joked. Why did my mother have to marry into a family of comedians?

"Can I see them?" I asked, pointedly ignoring both my stepbrothers.

"See what, honey?" Andy asked me.

For a moment I forgot what we were talking about. *Honey?* Andy had never called me *honey* before. What was going on here? Were we—I shudder to think it—*bonding?* Excuse me, I already have one father, even if he is dead. He still pops by to visit me all too often.

"I think she means the letters," my mother said, apparently not even noticing what her husband had just called me.

"Oh, sure," Andy said. "They're in our room."

"Our room" is the bedroom Andy and my mother sleep in. I try never to go in there, because, well, frankly, the whole thing grosses me out. Yeah, sure, I'm glad that my mom's finally happy, after ten years of mourning the death of my dad. But does that mean I want to actually *see* her in bed with her new husband, watching *The West Wing*? No thank you.

Still, after dinner, I steeled myself and went in there. My mom was at her dressing table taking off her makeup. She has to go to bed very early in order to be up in time for her stint on the morning news.

"Oh, hi, sweetie," my mom said to me in a dazed, I'm-busy kind of way. "They're over there, I think."

I looked where she pointed on top of Andy's dresser and found the metal box Dopey had dug up along with a lot of other guy-type stuff, like loose change and matches and receipts.

Anyway, Andy had tried to clean the box up, and he'd done a pretty good job of it. You could read almost all the writing on it.

Which was kind of unfortunate, because what the writing said was way politically incorrect. *Try new Red Injun cigars!* it urged. There was even a picture of this very proud-looking Native American clutching a fistful of cigars where his bow and quiver ought to have been. *The delicious aroma will tempt even the choosiest smoker. As with all our products, quality assured.*

That was it. No surgeon general's warning about how smoking can kill. Nothing about fetal birth weight. Still, it was kind of strange how advertising from before they had TV—before they even had *radio*—was still basically the same as advertising today. Only, you know, now we know that naming your product after a race of people will probably offend them.

I opened the box and found the letters inside. Andy was right about their poor condition. They were so yellowed that you could hardly peel them apart without having pieces crumble off. They had, I could see, been tied together with a ribbon, a silk one, which might have been another color once, but was now an ugly brown.

There was a stack of letters, maybe five or six in all, in the box. I can't tell you, as I picked up the first one, what I thought I'd see. But I guess a part of me knew all along what I was going to find.

Even so, when I'd carefully unfolded the first one and read the words *Dear Hector*, I still felt like somebody had snuck up behind me and kicked me.

I had to sit down. I sank down into one of the armchairs my mom and Andy keep by the fire-place in their room, my eyes still glued to the yel-lowed page in front of me.

Jesse. These letters were to Jesse.

"Suze?" My mom glanced at me curiously. She was rubbing cream into her face. "Are you all right?"

"Fine," I said in a strangled voice. "Is it okay . . . is it okay if I just sit here and read these for a minute?"

My mom began to slop cream onto her hands. "Of course," she said. "You're sure you're all right? You look a little . . . pale."

"I'm great," I lied. "Just great."

Dear Hector, the first letter said. The hand-writing was beautiful—loopy and old-fashioned, the kind of handwriting Sister Ernestine, back at school, used. I could read it quite easily, despite the fact that the letter was dated May 8, 1850.

1850! That was the year our house had been built, the first year it was in business as a boarding-house for travelers to the Monterey Peninsula area. The year—I knew from when Doc and I looked it up—that Jesse, or Hector (which is his real name; can you imagine? I mean, *Hector*) had mysteri-ously disappeared.

Though I happen to know there hadn't been anything mysterious about it. He'd been murdered in this very house . . . in fact, in my bedroom upstairs. Which is why, for the past century and a half, he's been hanging out there, waiting for . . .

Waiting for what?

Waiting for you, said a small voice in the back of my head. A mediator, to find these letters and avenge his death, so he can move on to wherever it is he's supposed to go next.

The thought struck me with terror. Really. It made my hands go all sweaty, even though it was cool in my mom and Andy's room, what with the air-conditioning being on full blast. The back of my neck started feeling prickly and gross.

I forced myself to look back down at the letter. If Jesse was meant to move on, well, then I was just going to have to help him do it. That's my job, after all.

Except that I couldn't help thinking about Father Dom. A fellow mediator, he had admitted to me a few months ago that he had once had the misfortune to fall in love with a ghost, back when he'd been my age. Things hadn't worked out— how could they?—and he'd become a priest.

Got that? A *priest*. Okay? That's how bad it had

been. That's how hard the loss had been to get over. *He'd become a priest.*

Frankly, I don't see how I could ever become a nun. For one thing, I'm not even Catholic. And for another, I don't look very good with my hair pulled back. Really. That's why I've always avoided ponytails and headbands.

Stop it, I said to myself. *Just stop it and read.*

I read.

The letter was from someone called Maria. I don't know much about Jesse's life before he died—he's not exactly big on discussing it—but I do know that Maria de Silva was the name of the girl Jesse had been on his way to marry when he'd disappeared. Some cousin of his. I'd seen a picture of her once in a book. She was pretty hot, you know, for a girl in a hoopskirt who lived before plastic surgery. Or Maybelline.

And you could tell by the way she wrote that she knew it, too. That she was hot, I mean. Her letter was all about the parties she'd been to, and who had said what about her new bonnet. Her *bonnet*, for crying out loud. I swear to God, it was like reading a letter from Kelly Prescott, except that it had a bunch of *hithers* and *alacks* in it, and no mention of Ricky Martin. Plus a lot of stuff was spelled wrong. Maria may have been a babe, but it was pretty clear, after reading her letters, she hadn't won too many spelling bees back at ye olde schoolhouse.

What struck me, as I read, was the fact that it really didn't seem possible that the girl who had written these letters was the same girl who had, I was pretty sure, ordered a hit on her fiancé. Because I happened to know that Maria hadn't wanted to marry Jesse at all. Her dad had arranged the whole thing. Maria had wanted to marry this other guy, this dude named Diego, who ran slaves for a living. A real charming guy. In fact, Diego was the one I suspected had killed Jesse.

Not, of course, that Jesse had ever mentioned any of this—or anything at all, for that matter, about his past. He is, and always has been, completely tight-lipped on the whole subject of how he'd died. Which I guess I can understand: Getting murdered has to be a bit traumatizing.

But I must say it's kind of hard getting to the bottom of why he's still here after all this time when he won't contribute at all to the conversation. I had had to find out all of this stuff from a book on the history of Salinas County that Doc had dug up out of the local library.

So I guess you could say that I read Maria's

letters with a certain sense of foreboding. I mean, I was pretty much convinced I was going to find something in them that was going to prove Jesse had been murdered . . . and who'd done it.

But the last letter was just as fatuous as the other four. There was nothing, nothing at all to indicate any wrongdoing of any kind on Maria's part . . . except for maybe a complete inability to spell the word fiancé. And really, what sort of crime is that?

I folded the letters carefully again and stuck them back into the tin, realizing, as I did so, that the back of my neck, as well as my hands, was no longer sweating. Was I relieved that there was nothing incriminating here, nothing that helped solve the mystery of Jesse's death?

I guess so. Selfish of me, I know, but it's the truth. All I knew now was what Maria de Silva had worn to some party at the Spanish ambassador's house. Big deal. Why would anybody stick letters as innocuous as that into a cigar box and bury them? It made no sense.

"Interesting, aren't they?" my mother said when I stood up.

I jumped about a mile. I'd forgotten she was even there. She was in bed now, reading a book on how to be a more effective time manager.

"Yeah," I said, putting the letters back on Andy's dresser. "Really interesting. I'm so glad I know what the ambassador's son said when he saw Maria de Silva in her new silver gauze ballgown."

My mom looked up at me curiously through the lenses of her reading glasses. "Oh, did she mention her last name somewhere? Because Andy and I were wondering. We didn't see it. De Silva, did you say?"

I blinked. "Um," I said. "No. Well, she didn't say. But Doc and I . . . I mean, David, he told me about this family, the de Silvas, that lived in Salinas around that time, and they had a daughter called Maria, and I just . . ." My voice trailed off as Andy came into the room.

"Hey, Suze," he said, looking a little surprised to see me in his room, since I'd never set foot in there before. "Did you see the letters? Neat, huh?"

Neat. Oh my God. Neat.

"Yeah," I said. "Gotta go. Good night."

I couldn't get out of there fast enough. I don't know how kids whose parents have been married multiple times deal with it. I mean, my mother's only remarried once, and to a perfectly nice man. But still, it's just so *weird*.

But if I'd thought I could retreat to my room to

be alone and think things over, I was wrong. Jesse was sitting on my window seat.

Sitting there looking like he always looked: totally hot, in the white open-necked shirt and black toreador pants he habitually wears—well, it's not like you can change clothes in the after-life—with his short dark hair curling crisply against the back of his neck, and his liquid black eyes bright beneath equally inky brows, one of which bore a thin white scar. . . .

A scar that, more times than I like to admit, I'd dreamed of tracing with my fingertips.

He looked up when I came in—he had Spike, my cat, on his lap—and said, "This book is very difficult to understand." He was reading a copy of *First Blood*, by David Morrell, which they based the movie *Rambo* on.

I blinked, trying to rouse myself from the dazed stupor the sight of him always seemed to put me in for a minute or so.

"If Sylvester Stallone understood it," I said, "I would think you could."

Jesse ignored that. "Marx predicted that the contradictions and weaknesses within the capital-ist structure would cause increasingly severe eco-nomic crises and deepening impoverishment of the working class," he said, "which would eventu-

ally revolt and seize control of the means of pro-
duction . . . which is precisely what happened in
Vietnam. What induced the U.S. government to
think that they were justified in involving themselves in the struggle of the people of this develop-
ing nation to find economic solidarity?"

My shoulders sagged. Really, is it too much to
ask that I be able to come home from a long day
of work and relax? Oh, no. I have to come home
and read a bunch of letters written to the love of
my life by his fiancée, who, if I am correct, had
him killed a hundred and fifty years ago.

Then, as if that is not bad enough, he wants me
to explain the Vietnam War.

I really have to start hiding my textbooks from
him. The thing is, he reads them and actually
manages to retain what they say, and then applies
that to other things he finds to read around the
house.

Why he can't just watch TV, like a normal person, I do not know.

I went over to my bed and collapsed onto it,
face-first. I was, I should mention, still wearing
my horrible shorts from the hotel. But I couldn't
bring myself to care what Jesse thought about the
size of my butt at that particular moment.

I guess it must have showed. Not my butt, I

mean, but my general unhappiness with the way my summer was going.

"Are you all right?" Jesse wanted to know.

"Yes," I said into my pillows.

Jesse said after a minute, "Well, you don't seem all right. Are you sure nothing is wrong?"

Yes, something is wrong, I wanted to shriek at him. I just spent twenty minutes reading a bunch of private correspondence from your ex-fiancée, and might I add that she seems like a terrifically *boring* individual? How could you have ever been stupid enough to have agreed to marry her? Her and her stupid *bonnet*?

But the thing is, I didn't want Jesse to know I'd read his mail. I mean, we're basically roommates and all, and there are certain things you just don't do. For instance, Jesse is always tactfully not around whenever I am changing and bathing and whatnot. And I am very careful to stock up on food and litter for Spike, who, unlike a normal animal, actually seems to prefer ghost company to human. He only tolerates me because I feed him.

Of course, Jesse has, in the past, felt no compunction about materializing in the backseats of cars in which I happened to have been making out with someone.

But I know Jesse would never read my mail, of which I get only a limited amount, mostly in the form of letters from my best friend, Gina, back in Brooklyn. And I have to admit, I felt guilty for reading his, even though it was more than a hundred and fifty years old and there certainly wouldn't have been anything about me in it.

What surprised me was that Jesse, who is, after all, a ghost, and can go anywhere without being seen—except by me and Father Dom, of course, and now, I guess, by Jack—didn't know about the letters. Really, he seemed to have no idea both that they'd been found and that, just moments before, I'd been downstairs, reading them.

But then, *First Blood* is pretty engrossing, I suppose.

So instead of telling him what was *really* wrong with me—you know, anything about the letters, and especially anything about the whole *I'm in love with you, only where can it go? Because you're not even alive and I'm the only one who can see you, and besides, it's clear you don't feel the same way about me. Do you? Well, do you?* thing—I just said, "Well, I met another mediator today, and I guess that kind of weirded me out."

And then I rolled over and told him about Jack. Jesse was very interested and told me I ought to call Father Dom with the news. What I wanted to do, of course, was call Father Dom and tell him about the letters. But I couldn't do that with Jesse in the room because, of course, he'd know I'd been prying in his personal affairs, which, given his whole secrecy thing about how he'd died, I doubted he'd appreciate.

So I said, "Good idea," and picked up the phone and dialed Father D.'s number.

Only Father D. didn't answer. Instead, a woman did. At first I freaked out, thinking Father Dominic was shacking up. But then I remembered that he lives in a rectory with a bunch of other people.

So I went, "Is Father Dominic there?" hoping it was only a novice or something and would go away and get him without comment.

But it wasn't a novice. It was Sister Ernestine, who is the assistant principal of my high school and who, of course, recognized my voice.

"Susannah Simon," she said. "What are you doing calling Father Dominic at home at this hour? Do you know what time it is, young lady? It is nearly ten o'clock!"

"I know," I said. "Only—"

"Besides, Father Dominic isn't here," Sister Ernestine went on. "He's on retreat."

"Retreat?" I echoed, picturing Father Dominic sitting in front of a campfire with a bunch of other priests, singing "Kumbaya My Lord" and possibly wearing sandals.

Then I remembered that Father Dominic had mentioned that he would be going on a retreat for the principals of Catholic high schools. He'd even given me the number there, in case there was some kind of ghost emergency and I needed to reach him. I didn't count discovering a new mediator as an emergency, however . . . though doubtless Father Dom would. So I just thanked Sister Ernestine, apologized for disturbing her, and hung up.

"What is a retreat?" Jesse wanted to know.

So then I explained to him what a retreat is, but the whole time I was sitting there thinking about the time he'd touched my face in the hospital and wondering if it had been because he just felt sorry for me or if he actually liked me (more than just as a friend—I know he likes me as a friend) or what.

Because the thing is, even though he's been dead for a hundred and fifty years, Jesse is really an extreme hottie—much hotter even than Paul Slater . . . or maybe I just think so because I'm in love with him.

But whatever. I mean, he really is like someone straight off the WB. He even has nice teeth for a guy born before they invented fluoride, very white and even and strong-looking. I mean, if there were any guys at the Mission Academy who looked even remotely like Jesse, going to school wouldn't seem at all like the massive waste of time it actually is.

But what good is it? I mean, him looking so good, and all? He's a *ghost*. I'm the only one who can see him. It's not like I'll ever be able to introduce him to my mother, or take him to the prom, or marry him, or whatever. *We have no future together.*

I have to remember that.

But sometimes it's really, really hard. Especially when he's sitting there in front of me, laughing at what I'm saying, and petting that stupid, smelly cat. Jesse was the first person I met when I moved to California, and he became my first real friend here. He has always been there when I needed him, which is way more than I can say for most of the living people I know. And if I had to choose one person to be marooned on a desert island with, I wouldn't even have to think about it: Of course it would be Jesse.

This is what I was thinking as I explained

about retreats. It was what I was thinking as I went on to explain what I knew about the Vietnam War, and then the eventual fall of communism in the former Soviet Union. It was what I was thinking as I brushed my teeth and got ready for bed. It was what I was thinking as I said good night to him and crawled under the covers and turned out the light. It was what I was thinking as sleep overcame me and blissfully blotted out all thought whatsoever . . . the time I spend sleeping being the only time, lately, when I can escape thoughts of Jesse.

But let me tell you, it came back in full force when, just a few hours later, I woke with a start to find a hand pressed over my mouth.

And, oh yeah, a knife held to my throat.

chapter *four*

Being a mediator, I am not unaccustomed to being woken in, shall we say, a less than gentle manner.

But this was a *lot* less gentle than usual. I mean, usually when someone wants your help, they go out of their way not to antagonize you . . . which waving a knife around has a tendency to do.

But as soon as I opened my eyes and saw who this knife-wielding individual was, I realized that probably what she wanted was not my help. No, probably what she wanted was to kill me.

Don't ask me how I knew. Undoubtedly those old mediator instincts at work.

Well and the knife was a pretty significant indicator.

"Listen to me, you stupid girl," Maria de Silva hissed at me. Maria de Silva *Diego*, I should say, since at the time of her death, she was married to Felix Diego, the slave-runner. I know all this from that book Doc got out of the library called *My Monterey*, a history of Salinas County from 1800 to 1850. There'd even been that portrait of Maria in it.

Which was how I happened to know who was trying to kill me this time.

"If," Maria hissed, "you don't get your father and brother to stop digging that hole"—um, *step-* father and *step*brother, I wanted to correct her, only I couldn't, on account of the hand over my mouth—"I'll make you sorry you were ever born. Got that?"

Pretty tough talk from a girl in a hoopskirt. Because that's what she was. A girl.

She hadn't been when she'd died. When she had died, around the turn of the century—last century, of course, not this one—Maria de Silva Diego had been around seventy or so.

But the ghost on top of me appeared to be my own age. Her hair was black, without a hint of gray, and she wore it in these very fancy ringlets on either side of her face. She appeared to have a lot going on in the jewelry department. There was this big fat ruby hanging from a gold chain around her long, slender neck—very *Titanic* and all—and she had some heavy-duty rings on her fingers. One of them was cutting into my gums.

That's the thing about ghosts, though—the thing that they always get wrong in the movies. When you die, your spirit does not take on the form your body had at the moment you croaked. You just don't ever see ghosts walking around with their guts spilling out, or their severed head in their hands, or whatever. If you did, Jack might have been justified in being such a little scaredy-cat.

But it doesn't happen that way. Instead, your ghost appears in the form your body had when you were at your most vital, your most alive.

And I guess for Maria de Silva, that was when she was sixteen or so.

Hey, it was nice she had an option, you know? Jesse hadn't been allowed to live long enough to have much of a choice. Thanks to her.

"Oh, no, you don't," Maria said, the backs of her rings scraping against my teeth in a manner I would really have to describe as unpleasant. "Don't even think about it."

I don't know how she'd known, but I had been

considering ramming my knees into her spine. The knife blade pressing against my jugular soon dissuaded me from that plan, however.

"You're going to make your father stop digging back there, and you're going to destroy those letters, understand, little girl?" Maria hissed. "And you aren't going to say a word about them—or me—to Hector. Am I making myself clear?"

What could I do? She had a *knife* to my throat. And there was nothing in her manner at all reminiscent of the Maria de Silva who'd written those idiotic letters. This chick was not gushing about her new bonnet, if you get my drift. I hadn't any doubt at all that she not only knew how to use that knife, but that she fully intended to do so, if provoked.

I nodded to show her that I was perfectly willing, under the circumstances, to follow her orders.

"Good," Maria de Silva said. And then she lifted her fingers from my mouth. I could taste blood.

She had straddled me—which accounted for all the lacy petticoat in my face, tickling my nose—and now she looked down at me, her pretty features twisted into an expression of disgust.

"And they said for me to look out," she sneered.

"That you were a tricky one. But you aren't so tricky, are you? You're just a girl. A stupid little girl."

She threw back her head and laughed.

And then she was gone. Just like that.

As soon as I felt like I could move again, I got out of bed and went into my bathroom, where I turned on the light and looked at my reflection in the mirror above my sink.

No. It hadn't been a nightmare. There was blood between my teeth where Maria de Silva's ring had cut into me.

I rinsed until all the blood was gone, then turned off the bathroom light and came back into my room. I think I was in a daze or something. I couldn't quite register what had just happened. Maria de Silva. Maria de Silva, Jesse's fiancée—I think it would be safe to say ex-fiancée, under the circumstances—had just appeared in my room and threatened me. *Me*. Sweet little old *me*.

It was a lot to process, especially considering it was, oh, I don't know, four in the morning?

And yet it turned out I was in for yet another late-night shock. No sooner had I stepped from the bathroom than I noticed someone was leaning against one of the posts to the canopy over my bed.

Only it wasn't just someone, it was Jesse. And when he saw me, he straightened up.

"Are you all right?" he asked worriedly. "I thought I . . . Susannah, was somebody just here?"

Uh, your knife-wielding ex-girlfriend, you mean?

That's what I thought. What I said was, "No."

Okay. Don't start with me. The reason I didn't tell him had nothing to do with Maria's threat.

No, it was the other thing Maria had said. About telling Andy to quit digging in the backyard. Because that could mean only one thing: that there was something buried in the backyard Maria didn't want anybody to find.

And I had a feeling I knew what that something was.

I also had a feeling that that something was the reason Jesse had been hanging around the Carmel Hills for so long.

I should have blurted this all out to Jesse, right? I mean, come on: He had a right to know. It was something that very directly concerned him.

But it was also something that, I was fairly sure, was going to take him away from me forever.

Yeah, I know: If I really loved him, I'd have been willing to set him free, like in that poem that's always on those posters with the seagulls flying in the wind: *If you love something, set it free. If it was meant to be, it will come back to you.*

Let me tell you something. That poem is stupid, all right? And it so totally does not apply in this situation. Because once Jesse gets set free, he is never coming back to me. Because he won't be able to. Because he'll be in heaven, or another life, or whatever.

And then I'll have to become a nun.

God. *God*, everything sucks.

I crawled back into bed.

"Look, Jesse," I said, pulling the covers up to my chin. I had on a T-shirt and boxers, but, you know, no bra or anything. Not that he could tell, in the dark and all, but you never know. "I'm really tired."

"Oh," he said. "Of course. But . . . You're sure there wasn't anyone in here? Because I could swear I—"

I waited expectantly for him to finish. Just how would he end that sentence? *I could swear I heard the sweet dulcet tones of the woman I once loved? I could swear I smelled her perfume*—which, by the way, was of orange blossoms?

But he didn't say either of those things. Instead, looking really confused, he said, "Sorry," and disappeared, exactly the way his ex-girlfriend had disappeared. In fact, you'd think they might have run into each other, wouldn't you, out there on the spiritual plane, with all of this materializing and dematerializing?

But apparently not.

I won't lie and tell you that I dropped back off to sleep right away. I didn't. I was really, really tired, but my mind just kept repeating what Maria had said, over and over. What on earth was she so hot and bothered about, anyway? Those letters didn't have anything the least bit incriminating in them. I mean, if it's true that she had Jesse iced so she could marry her boyfriend Diego instead of him.

And if those letters were so important, why hadn't she had them destroyed properly all those years ago? Why were they buried in our backyard in a cigar tin?

But that wasn't what was really bothering me. What really bothered me was the fact that she wanted me to get Andy to stop digging altogether. Because that could only mean one thing:

There was something even more incriminating back there.

Like a body.

And I didn't even want to *think* about whose.

And when I woke up again a few hours later, after finally managing to nod off, I still didn't want to think about it.

But one thing I did know: I was not going to ask Andy to stop digging (like he'd even listen to me if I did), nor was I going to destroy those letters. No freaking way.

In fact, I took personal possession of them, just in case, telling Andy that I'd deliver them to the historical society myself. I figured they'd be safe there, in case old Maria Diego got up to anything. Andy looked surprised, but not enough actually to ask me what I was up to. He was too busy yelling at Dopey for shoveling in the wrong place.

When I got to the Pebble Beach Hotel and Golf Resort that morning, it was to be greeted by Caitlin with an accusatory, "Well, I don't know what you did to Jack Slater, but his family asked that you be assigned to watch him for the rest of their stay . . . until Sunday, actually."

I wasn't surprised. Nor did I mind, particularly. The Paul factor was troubling, of course, but now that I knew the reason behind Jack's odd behavior, I genuinely liked the kid.

And he, it became clear the moment I set foot inside his family's suite, was wild about me. No more lying on the floor in front of the TV for him. Jack was in his swimsuit and ready to go.

"Can you teach me the butterfly today, Suze?" he wanted to know. "I've always wanted to know how to do the butterfly."

"Susan," his mother said to me, in a whispered aside, right before she ran off to her hair appointment (neither Paul nor his father were around, much to my relief, having had a 7:00 tee time). "I can't thank you enough for what you've done for Jack. I don't know what you said to him yesterday, but he is like a different child. I have never seen him so happy. You know, he really is the most remarkably sensitive person. Such an imagination, too. Always thinking he's seeing . . . well, dead people. Has he mentioned this to you?"

I said nonchalantly that he had.

"Well, we've been at our wits' end. We must have had thirty different doctors look at him, and no one—*no one*—seemed able to get through to him. Then you came along, and . . . " Nancy Slater looked down at me with carefully made-up blue eyes. "Well, I don't know how we'll ever be able to thank you, Susan."

You could start, I thought, *by calling me by my right name*. But I didn't really care. I just said, "No problem, Mrs. Slater," and went and got Jack and headed with him back to the pool.

Jack *was* like a different kid. There was no denying that. Even Sleepy, roused from his semi-permanent doze by Jack's happy splashing, asked me if that was the same boy he'd seen me with the morning before, and when I told him it was, actually looked incredulous for a second or two before going back to sleep. The things that had once frightened Jack—basically, everything—no longer seemed to bother him in the least.

And so when, after burgers at the Pool House, I suggested he and I take the hotel shuttle bus into town, he didn't even protest. He even commented that the plan "sounded like fun."

Fun. From Jack. Really, maybe mediating isn't my calling at all. Maybe I should be a teacher, or a child psychologist, or something. Seriously.

Jack wasn't particularly thrilled, however, when, once we got into town, we headed toward the building that houses the Carmel-by-the-Sea Historical Society. He wanted to go to the beach, but when I told him that it was to help a ghost and that we'd go to the beach afterward, he was okay with it.

I'm not really a historical society type of gal, but even I have to admit it was kind of cool, looking at all the old photos on the walls of the place, photos of Carmel and Salinas County a hundred years earlier, before all the strip malls and Safeways opened, when it was all just fields dotted with cypress trees, like in that book they made us read in the eighth grade, *The Red Pony*. They had some pretty cool stuff there—not much, really, from Jesse's time, but a lot from later on, like after the Civil War. Jack and I were admiring something called a stereo viewer, which is what people used for entertainment before movies, when this untidy-looking bald man came out of his office and peered at us through glasses with lenses as thick as Coke bottle bottoms and said, "Yes, you wanted to see me?"

I said we wanted to see someone in charge. He said that was him, and introduced himself as Dr. Clive Clemmings, Ph.D. So I told Dr. Clive Clemmings, Ph.D., who I was and where I lived, and took the cigar tin from my JanSport backpack (Kate Spade really doesn't go with pleat-front khaki shorts) and showed him the letters. . . .

And he freaked out.

I mean it. He *freaked out*. He was so excited, he told the old lady at the reception desk to hold his calls (she looked up, astonished, from the romance novel she was reading; it was clear that Dr. Clive Clemmings, Ph.D., must not get many calls) and ushered Jack and me back into his private office. . . .

Where I nearly had a coronary. Because there, above Clive Clemmings's desk, was Maria de Silva's portrait, the one I had seen in that book Doc had taken out of the library.

The painter had done, I realized, an extraordinarily good job. He'd gotten it completely right, down to the artfully ringleted hair and the gold-and-ruby necklace around her elegantly curved neck, not to mention her snooty expression. . . .

"That's her!" I cried, completely involuntarily, stabbing my finger at the painting.

Jack looked up at me as if I'd gone mental—which I suppose I momentarily had—but Clive Clemmings only glanced over his shoulder at the portrait and said, "Yes, Maria Diego. Quite the jewel in the crown of our collection, that painting. Rescued it from being sold at a *garage sale* by one of her grandchildren, can you imagine? Down on his luck, poor old fellow. Disgraceful, when you think about it. None of the Diegos ever amounted to much, however. You know what they say about bad blood. And Felix Diego—"

Dr. Clive had opened the cigar tin and, using some special tweezery-looking things, unfolded the first letter. "Oh, my," he breathed, looking down at it.

"Yeah," I said. "It's from her." I nodded up at the painting. "Maria de Silva. It's a bunch of letters she wrote to Jesse—I mean, to Hector de Silva, her cousin, who she was supposed to marry, only he—"

"Disappeared." Clive Clemmings stared at me. He had to be, if I guessed, in his thirties or so— despite the very wide spot of bare scalp along the top of his head—and though by no means attractive, he did not look so utterly repulsive just then as he had before. A look of total astonishment, which certainly does not become many, did wonders for him.

"My God," he said. "*Where* did you find these?"

And so I told him again, and he got even more excited, and told us to wait in his office while he went and got something.

So we waited. Jack was very good while we did so. He only said, "When can we go to the beach already?" twice.

When Dr. Clive Clemmings, Ph.D., came back, he was holding a tray and a bunch of latex gloves, which he told us we had to put on if we were going to touch anything. Jack was pretty bored by that time, so he elected to go back out into the main room to play with the stereo viewer some more. Only I donned the gloves.

But was I glad I did. Because what Clive Clemmings let me touch when I had them on was everything the historical society had collected over the years that had anything whatsoever to do with Maria de Silva.

Which was, let me tell you, quite a lot.

But the things in the collection that most interested me were a tiny painting—a miniature, Clive Clemmings said it was called—of Jesse (or Hector de Silva, as Dr. Clive referred to him; apparently only Jesse's immediate family ever called him Jesse . . . his family, and me, of course) and five letters, in much better condition than the ones from the cigar box.

The miniature was perfect, like a little photograph. People could really paint back in those days, I guess. It was totally Jesse. It captured him perfectly. He had on that look he gets when I'm telling him about some great conquest I had made at an outlet—you know, scoring a Prada handbag for fifty percent off, or something. Like he couldn't care less.

In the painting, which was just of Jesse's head and shoulders, he was wearing something Clive Clemmings called a cravat, which was supposedly something all the guys wore back then, this big frilly white thing that wrapped around the neck a few times. It would have looked ridiculous on Dopey or Sleepy or even Clive Clemmings, in spite of his Ph.D.

But on Jesse, of course, it looked great.

Well, what wouldn't?

The letters were almost better than the painting, though, in a way. That's because they were all addressed to Maria de Silva . . . and signed by someone named Hector.

I pored over them, and I can't say that at the time I felt a lick of guilt about it, either. They were much more interesting than Maria's letters—although, like hers, not the least romantic. No, Jesse just wrote—very wittily, I might add—about the goings-on at his family's ranch and the funny things his sisters did. (It turns out he had five of them. Sisters, I mean. All younger, ranging in age, the year Jesse died, from sixteen to six. But had he ever mentioned this to me before? Oh, please.) There was also some stuff about local politics and how hard it was to keep good ranch hands on the job what with the gold rush on and all of them hurrying off to stake claims.

The thing was, the way Jesse wrote, you could practically hear him saying all this stuff. It was all very friendly and chatty and nice. Much better than Maria's braggy letters.

And nothing was spelled wrong, either.

As I read through Jesse's letters, Dr. Clive rattled on about how now that he had Maria's letters to Hector, he was going to add them to this exhibit he was planning for the fall tourist season, an exhibit on the whole de Silva clan and their importance to the growth of Salinas County over the years.

"If only," he said wistfully, "there were any of them left alive. De Silvas, I mean. It would be lovely to have them as guest speakers."

This got my attention. "There have to be some left," I said. "Didn't Maria and that Diego guy have like thirty-seven kids or something?"

Clive Clemmings looked stern. As a historian—and especially a Ph.D.—he did not seem to appreciate exaggeration of any kind.

"They had eleven children," he corrected me. "And they are not, strictly, de Silvas, but Diegos. The de Silva family unfortunately ran very strongly to daughters. I'm afraid Hector de Silva was the last male in the line. And of course we'll never know if he sired any male offspring. If he did, it certainly wasn't in northern California."

"Of course he didn't," I said, perhaps more

defensively than I ought to have. But I was peeved. Aside from the obvious sexism of the whole last-male-in-the-line thing, I took issue with the guy's assumption that Jesse might have been off procreating somewhere when, in fact, he had been foully murdered. "He was killed right in my own house!"

Clive Clemmings looked at me with raised eyebrows. It was only then that I realized what I had said.

"Hector de Silva," Dr. Clive said, sounding a lot like Sister Ernestine when we grew restless during the *begats* in Religion class, "disappeared shortly before his wedding to his cousin Maria and was never heard from again."

I couldn't very well sit there and go, *Yeah, but his ghost lives in my bedroom, and he told me* . . .

Instead, I said, "I thought the, um, perception was that Maria had her boyfriend, that Diego dude, kill Hector so she didn't have to marry him."

Clive Clemmings looked annoyed. "That is only a theory put forward by my grandfather, Colonel Harold Clemmings, who wrote—"

"*My Monterey*," I finished for him. "Yeah, that's what I meant. That guy's your grandfather?"

"Yes," Dr. Clive said, but he didn't look too

happy about it. "He passed away a good many years ago. And I can't say that I agree with his theory, Miss, er, Ackerman." I had donated Maria's letters in my stepfather's name, so Dr. Clive, sexist thing that he was, assumed that that was my name, too. "Nor can I say that his book sold at all well. My grandfather was extremely interested in the history of his community, but he was not an educated man, like me. He did not possess even a B.A., let alone a Ph.D. It has always been my belief—not to mention that of most local historians, with the sole exception of my grandfather—that young Mr. de Silva developed what is commonly referred to as 'cold feet'"—Dr. Clive made little quotation marks in the air with his fingers—"a few days before the wedding and, unable to face his family's embarrassment over his jilting the young woman in such a manner, went off in search of a claim of his own, perhaps near San Francisco. . . ."

It's amazing, but for a moment I actually envisioned sinking those tweezy things Clive Clemmings had made me use to turn the pages of Jesse's letters straight into his eyes. If I could have got them past the lenses of those goobery glasses, that is.

Instead, I pulled myself together and said, with

all the dignity I could muster while sitting there in a pair of khaki shorts with pleats down the front, "And do you really believe, in your heart of hearts, Clive, that the person who wrote these letters would do something like that? Go away without a word to his family? To his little sisters, whom he clearly loved, and about whom he wrote so affectionately? Do you really think that the reason these letters turned up in my backyard is because *he* buried them there? Or do you find it beyond the realm of possibility that the reason they turned up there is because *he's* buried there somewhere, and if my stepfather digs deep enough, he just might find him?"

My voice had risen shrilly. I supposed I was getting a little hysterical over the whole thing. So sue me.

"Will that make you see that your grandfather was a *hundred percent right*?" I shrieked. "When my stepfather finds Hector de Silva's *rotting corpse*?"

Clive Clemmings looked more astonished than ever before. "My dear Miss Ackerman!" he cried.

I think he said this because he'd realized, at the exact same moment as I had, that I was crying.

Which was actually pretty strange, because I am not a crier. I mean, yeah, sure, I cry when I bang my head on one of the kitchen cabinet doors or see one of those drippy Kodak commercials or whatever. But I don't, you know, go around weeping at the drop of a hat.

But there I was, sitting in the office of Dr. Clive Clemmings, Ph.D., bawling my eyes out. Good going, Suze. Real professional. Way to show Jack how to mediate.

"Well," I said in a shaky voice as I stripped off my latex gloves and stood up, "allow me to assure you, Clive, that you are very, very wrong. Jesse— I mean Hector—would never do something like that. That might be what *she* wants you to believe"—I nodded toward the painting above our heads, the sight of which I was now beginning to hate with a sort of passion—"but it isn't the truth. Jesse—I mean, Hector—isn't . . . *wasn't* like that. If he'd gotten 'cold feet' like you say"—I made the same stupid quotation marks in the air—"then he'd have called the whole thing off. And, yeah, his family might have been embarrassed, but they'd have forgiven him, because they clearly loved him as much as he loved them, and—"

But then I couldn't talk anymore, because I was crying so hard. It was maddening. I couldn't believe it. Crying. *Crying* in front of this clown.

So instead I turned around and stormed out of the room.

Not very dignified, I guess, considering that the last thing Dr. Clive Clemmings, Ph.D., saw of me was my butt, which must have looked enormous in those stupid shorts.

But I got the point across.

I think.

Of course, in the end, it turned out not to matter. But at the time, I had no way of knowing that.

And neither, unfortunately, did poor Dr. Clive Clemmings, Ph.D.

chapter *five*

God, I hate crying. It's so humiliating. And I swear I hardly ever do it.

I guess, though, that the stress of being assaulted in the dead of night by the knife-wielding ex-girlfriend of the guy I love, finally got to me. I pretty much didn't stop crying until Jack, in desperation, bought me a Yoo-hoo from Jimmy's Quick Mart on our way down to the beach.

That and a Butterfinger bar soon had me feeling like myself again, and it wasn't long before Jack and I were frolicking in the waves, making fun of the tourists, and placing penny bets on which surfer would be knocked off his board first. We had such a good time that it wasn't until the sun started setting that I realized I had to get Jack back to the hotel.

Not that anybody had missed us, we discovered when we got there. As I dropped Jack off at his family's suite, his mother popped her head in from the terrace, where she and Dr. Rick were enjoying cocktails, and said, "Oh, it's you, is it, Jack? Hurry and change for dinner, will you? We're meeting the Robertsons. Thank you, Susan, and see you in the morning."

I waved and left, relieved that I'd managed to avoid Paul. After my unexpectedly traumatic afternoon, I did not think I could handle a confrontation with Mr. Tennis Whites.

But my relief turned out to be precipitous. As I was sitting in the front seat of the Land Rover, waiting for Sleepy to tear himself away from Caitlin, who seemed to have something terribly urgent to discuss with him just as we were leaving, someone tapped on my rolled-up window. I looked around, and there was Paul, wearing a *tie*, of all things, and a dark blue sports jacket.

I pushed the button that rolled the window down.

"Um," I said. "Hi."

"Hi," he said. He was smiling pleasantly. The last of the day's sunlight picked up the gold highlights in his brown curls. He really was, I had to admit, good-looking. Kelly Prescott would have eaten him up with a spoon. "I suppose you already have plans for tonight," he said.

I didn't, of course, but I replied quickly, "Yes."

"I figured." His smile was still pleasant. "What about tomorrow night?"

Look, I know I'm a freak, all right? You don't have to tell me. There I was, and this totally hot, totally nice guy was asking me out, and all I could think about was a guy who, let's face it, is dead. All right? *Jesse is dead.* It's stupid—stupid, stupid, *stupid*—of me to turn down a date with a live guy when the only other guy I have in my life is dead.

But that's exactly what I did. I went, "Gee, sorry, Paul. I have plans tomorrow night, too."

I didn't even care if it sounded like I was lying. That's how screwed up I am. I just could not drum up the slightest bit of interest.

But I guess that was a pretty big mistake. I guess Mr. Paul Slater isn't used to girls turning down his invitations to dinner, or whatever. Because he went, no longer smiling pleasantly—or at all, actually: "Well, that's too bad. It's especially too bad considering the fact that now I guess I'm going to have to tell your supervisor about how you took my little brother off hotel property today without my parents' permission."

I just stared at him through the open window. I couldn't even figure out what he was talking about, at first. Then I remembered the shuttle bus, and the historical society, and the beach.

I almost burst out laughing. Seriously. I mean, if Paul Slater thought my getting in trouble for taking a kid off hotel property without his parents' permission was the worst thing that could happen to me—that had even happened to me *today*—he was way, way off base. For crying out loud, a woman who'd been been dead for nearly a hundred years had held a knife to my throat in my own bedroom, not twenty-four hours earlier. Did he really think I was going to care if *Caitlin* issued me a *reprimand*?

"Go ahead," I said. "And when you tell her, be sure to mention that for the first time in his life, your brother actually had a good time."

I hit the button to roll up the window—I mean, really, what was this guy's damage?—but Paul stuck his hand through it and rested his fingers on the glass. I let go of the button. I mean, I just wanted him to go away, not get maimed for life.

"Yeah," Paul said. "I've been meaning to ask you about that. Jack tells me that you told him he's a medium."

"Mediator," I corrected him before I could stop myself. And so much for Jack keeping the whole thing a secret, like I'd advised him to. When was this kid going to learn that going around telling people he can talk to ghosts wasn't going to endear him to anyone?

"Whatever," Paul said. "I guess you must think making fun of someone who has a mental disorder is pretty amusing."

I couldn't believe it. I really couldn't. It was like something out of a TV show. Not on the WB, though, or even Fox. It was totally PAX.

"I do not think your brother has a mental disorder," I said.

"Oh, don't you?" Paul looked all knowing. "He tells you he sees dead people, and you think he's playing with a full deck?"

I shook my head. "Jack might be able to see dead people, Paul. You don't know. I mean, you can't prove he *can't* see dead people."

Oh, brilliant argument, Suze. Where the hell was Sleepy? Come on, already. Get me out of here.

"Suze," Paul said, looking at me all searchingly. "Please. Dead people? You really believe that? You really believe my brother can see—can speak to—the dead?"

"I've heard of weirder things," I said. I glanced

over at Sleepy. Caitlin was smiling up at him and shaking her blond Jennifer Aniston mane all over the place. Oh my God, enough with the flirting already. Just ask him out and get it over with so I can go . . .

"Yeah, well, you shouldn't be encouraging him," Paul said. "It's about the worst thing you can do, according to his doctors."

"Yeah?" I was getting kind of pissed off now. I mean, what did Paul Slater know about anything, anyway? Just because his father's a brain surgeon or whatever who can afford a week at the Pebble Beach Hotel and Golf Resort doesn't make him right all the time. "Well, Jack seems fine to me. You might even learn a thing or two from him, Paul. At least he has an open mind."

Paul just shook his head in disbelief. "What are you saying, Suze? That *you* believe in ghosts?"

Finally, *finally*, Sleepy said good-bye to Caitlin and turned back toward the car.

"Yeah," I said. "I do. What about you, Paul?"

Paul just blinked at me. "What about me?"

"Do you believe?"

His curled upper lip was all the reply I needed. Not caring if I severed his hand, I hit the window button. Paul pulled his fingers out just in time. I guess he thought I wasn't the finger-severing type.

Was he ever wrong.

Why are boys so difficult? I mean, really. When they aren't drinking directly out of the carton or leaving the toilet seat up, they are getting all offended because you won't go out with them and threatening to rat you out to your supervisor. Hasn't it occurred to any of them that this is not the way to our hearts?

And the problem is, they are just going to keep on doing it, as long as stupid girls like Kelly Prescott keep agreeing to go out with them anyway, in spite of their defects.

I sulked all the way home. Even Sleepy noticed.

"What's with you?" he wanted to know.

"That stupid Paul Slater's mad because I won't go out with him," I said, even though I generally make it a policy not to share my personal problems with any of my stepbrothers except, occasionally, Doc, and then only because his IQ is so much higher than mine. "He says he's going to tell Caitlin I took his little brother off hotel property without his parents' permission, which I did, but only to take him to the beach." And to the Carmel Historical Society. But I didn't mention that.

Sleepy went, "No kidding? That's pretty low.

Well, don't worry about it. I'll smooth things over with Caitlin for you, if you want."

I was shocked. I had only mentioned it because I was feeling so down in the dumps. I hadn't actually expected Sleepy to *help*, or anything.

"Really? You really will?"

"Sure," Sleepy said with a shrug. "I'm seeing her tonight after I get off from delivering." Sleepy lifeguards by day and delivers pizzas by night. Originally he was saving up for a Camaro. Now he is saving up to get his own apartment, since there are no dorms at the community college he'll be attending, and Andy says he isn't going to pay for Sleepy to have his own place unless he pulls his grades up.

I couldn't believe it. I said, "Thanks," in a stunned way.

"What's wrong with that Slater guy, anyway?" Sleepy wanted to know. "I thought he'd be just your type. You know, smart and all."

"Nothing's wrong with him," I grumbled, fiddling with my seat belt. "I just . . . I sort of like someone else."

Sleepy lifted up his eyebrows behind his Ray-Bans. "Oh? Anyone I know?"

I said shortly, "No."

"I don't know, Suze," he said. "Try me. Between

the pizza gig and school, I know most everybody."

"You definitely," I said, "do not know this guy."

Sleepy frowned. "Why? Is he some kind of gangbanger?"

I rolled my eyes. Sleepy has been convinced since almost the day we first met that I am in a gang. Seriously. As if gang members wear Stila. I am so sure.

"Does he live in the Valley?" Sleepy wanted to know. "Suze, I'm telling you right now, if I find out you're going out with a gangbanger from the Valley—"

"God!" I yelled. "Would you stop? He isn't a gangbanger, and neither am I! And he doesn't live in the Valley. You don't know him, okay? Just forget we had this conversation."

See? See what I mean? See why things will never, ever work out between me and Jesse? Because I can't pull him out and go, *Here he is, this is the guy I like, and he isn't a gangbanger, and he doesn't live in the Valley.*

I have just got to learn to keep my mouth shut, same as Jack.

When we got home, we were informed that dinner wasn't ready yet. That was because Andy was waist-deep in the hole he and Dopey had made in the backyard. I went out and looked at it for a while, chewing on my thumbnail. It was very creepy, looking into that hole. Almost as creepy as the prospect of going to bed in a few hours, knowing that Maria was probably going to show up again.

And that, seeing as how I hadn't done a single thing she'd asked, this time she'd probably cut up a lot more than just my gums.

It was around then that the phone rang. It was my friend CeeCee, wanting to know if I cared to join her and Adam McTavish at the Coffee Clutch to drink iced tea and talk bad about everyone we know. I said yes right away because I hadn't heard from either of them in so long. CeeCee was doing a summer internship at the *Carmel Pine Cone* (the name of the local newspaper; can you imagine?) and Adam had been at his grandparents' house in Martha's Vineyard for most of the summer. The minute I heard her voice I realized how much I'd missed CeeCee, and how great it would be to tell her about vile Paul Slater and his tricks.

But then, of course, I realized I'd have to tell her the part about Paul's little brother, and how he really can speak to the dead, or the story wouldn't have half as much pathos, and the fact is, CeeCee is not the type who believes in ghosts, or anything, for that matter, that she can't see with her own two eyes, which makes the fact that she goes to Catholic school problematic, what with Sister Ernestine urging us all the time about faith and the Holy Spirit.

But whatever. It was better than standing around at home, looking at a giant hole.

I hurried upstairs and slipped out of my uniform and into one of the cute J. Crew slip dresses I'd ordered and never gotten a chance to wear since I've spent the whole summer in my heinous khaki shorts. No sign of Jesse, but that was just as well, as I wouldn't have known what to say to him anyway. I felt totally guilty for having read his letters, even though at the same time I was glad I had done it, because knowing about his sisters and his problems on the ranch and all made me feel closer to him in a way.

Only it was a fake kind of close because he didn't know I knew. And if he had wanted me to know, don't you think he would have told me? But he never wants to talk about himself. Instead, he always wants to talk about things like the rise of the Third Reich and how could we as a country have possibly sat around and let six million Jews get gassed before doing anything about it?

You know. Things like that.

Actually, some of the things Jesse wants to discuss are very hard to explain. I'd much rather talk about his sisters. For instance, had he found living with five girls as trying as I find living with three boys? I would imagine probably not, given the reverse toilet seat situation. Did they even have toilets back then? Or did they just go in those nasty outhouses, like on *Little House on the Prairie*?

God, no wonder Maria was in such a bad mood.

Well, that and the whole being dead thing.

Anyway, Mom and Andy let me go out to eat with my friends because there was nothing for dinner anyway. Family meals really weren't the same, anyway, without Doc. I was surprised to find that I actually missed him and couldn't wait for him to come home. He was the only one of my stepbrothers who did not enrage me on any sort of regular basis.

Even though I couldn't really tell CeeCee about Paul, I did have a good time. It was good to see her, and Adam, who, of all the boys I know, acts the least like one, though he isn't gay or anything, and actually takes great umbrage if you suggest it. So does CeeCee, who has been in love with Adam since, like, forever. I had great hopes that

Adam might return her feelings, but I could tell things had kind of cooled off—at least on his part—since he'd been away.

As soon as he got up to go to the bathroom, I asked CeeCee what was up with that, and she launched into this whole thing about how she thinks Adam met someone in Martha's Vineyard. I have to say, it was kind of nice listening to someone else complain for a while. I mean, my life pretty much sucks and all, but at least I know Jesse's not screwing around on me with some girl in Martha's Vineyard.

At least, I don't think so. Who knows where he goes when he isn't hanging around my room? It could be Martha's Vineyard, after all.

See? See how this relationship is never going to work?

Anyway, CeeCee and Adam and I hadn't seen each other in a long time, so there were quite a few people we needed to say bad things about, primarily Kelly Prescott, so when I got home, it was almost eleven . . . late for me, what with my having to be at work by eight.

Still, I was glad I'd gone out, as it had taken my mind off what I suspected awaited me in a few hours: another visit from the ravishing Mrs. Diego.

But as I was washing my hair before bed, it occurred to me that there was no reason why I had to make things easy on Miss Maria. I mean, why should I be victimized in my own bed?

No reason. No reason at all. I did not have to put up with that kind of nonsense. Because that's what it was. Nonsense.

Well, sort of scary nonsense, but still nonsense, all the same.

So when I turned out the light that night, it was with a definite sense of satisfaction. I was, I felt, well protected from anything Maria might pull. I had with me beneath the covers a veritable arsenal of weapons, including an ax, a hammer, and something I could not identify that I had taken from Andy's workshop, but which had evil-looking spikes on it. Furthermore, I had Max the dog with me. He would, I knew, awaken me as soon as anything otherworldly showed up, being extremely sensitive to such things.

And, oh, yes, I slept in Doc's room.

I know. I know. Cowardly in the extreme. But why should I have stayed in my own bed and waited for her, like a lame duck, when I could sleep in Doc's bed and maybe throw her off the scent? I mean, it wasn't like I was looking for a fight or anything. Well, except for the whole not-doing-a-thing-she-said thing. I guess that was sort of indicative of looking for a fight. But not, you know, actively.

Because, I have to tell you, while ordinarily I might have gone out looking for Maria de Silva's grave, so I could just, you know, have it out with her then and there, this was a little different. Because of Jesse. Don't ask me why, but I just didn't think I had it in me to go and rough up his ex, the way I would have if she didn't have this connection to him. I can't say I'm really used to waiting for ghosts to come to me. . . .

But this. This was different.

Anyway, I had just snuggled down between Doc's sheets (freshly laundered—I wasn't taking any chances. I don't know what goes on in the beds of twelve-year-old boys, and frankly, I don't want to know) and was blinking in the darkness at the odd things Doc has hanging from his ceiling, a model of the solar system and all of that, when Max started to growl.

He did it so low that at first I didn't hear it. But since I had pulled him into bed with me (not that there was a lot of room, what with the ax and the hammer and the spiky thing) I could *feel* the growl reverberating through his big canine chest.

Then it got louder, and the hair on Max's back

started standing up. That's when I knew we were in for either an earthquake or a nocturnal visitation from the former belle of Salinas County.

I sat up, grabbing the spiky thing and holding it like a baseball bat, looking around wildly while saying to Max in a low voice, "Good boy. It's okay, boy. Everything's going to be all right, boy," and telling myself that I believed it.

That's when someone materialized in front of me. And I swung the spiky thing as I hard as I could.

chapter *six*

"Susannah!" Jesse cried from where he'd leaped to avoid being struck. "What are you *doing*?"

I nearly dropped the spiky thing, I was so relieved it was him.

Max went wild with whining and growling. The poor thing was clearly having some sort of doggie nervous breakdown. In order not to risk his waking everyone in the house, and then having to explain why I was sleeping in my stepbrother's bed with a bunch of Andy's tools, I let him out of the room. As I did so, Jesse took the spiky thing from me and looked down at it curiously.

"Susannah," he said when I'd closed the door again, "why are you sleeping in David's room, armed with a pick?"

I raised my eyebrows, looking way more surprised than the occasion warranted. "Is *that* what that is? I was wondering."

Jesse just shook his head at me. "Susannah," he said, "tell me what is going on. Now."

"Nothing," I said, my voice sounding too squeaky and high-pitched even to my own ears. I hurried forward and got back into Doc's bed, stubbing my toe on the hammer but not saying anything, since I didn't want Jesse to know it was there. Finding me in my stepbrother's bed with a pick was one thing. Finding me in my stepbrother's bed with a pick, an ax, and a hammer was something else entirely.

"Susannah." Jesse sounded really mad, and he doesn't get mad all that often. Except, of course, when he finds me sucking face with strange boys in the driveway, that is. "Is that an *ax*?"

Damn! I shoved it back down beneath the covers. "I can explain," I said.

He leaned the pick against the side of the bed and folded his arms across his chest. "I'd like to hear it," he said.

"Well." I took a deep breath. "It's like this."

And then I couldn't think of any way to explain it, other than the truth.

And I couldn't tell him that.

Jesse must have read in my face the fact that I was trying to think up a lie, since he suddenly unfolded his arms and leaned forward, placing one hand on either side of the headboard behind me, and sort of capturing me between his arms, though he wasn't actually touching me. This was very unnerving and caused me to slump down very low against Doc's pillows.

But even that didn't really do any good, since Jesse's face was still only about six inches from mine.

"Susannah," he said. He was *really* mad now. Fed up, even, you might say. "What is happening here? Last night I could swear I felt . . . a presence in your room. And then tonight you are sleeping in here, with picks and axes? What is it that you aren't telling me? And why? Why can't you tell me?"

I had sunk down as low as I could, but there was no escaping Jesse's angry face, unless I threw the sheet up over my head. And that, of course, wouldn't be at all dignified.

"Look," I said as reasonably as I could, considering that there was a hammer digging into my foot. "It's not that I don't want to tell you. It's just that I'm afraid that if I do . . . "

And then, don't ask me how, the whole thing just came tumbling out. Really. It was incredible. It was like he'd pushed a button on my forehead that said Information Please, and out it all came.

I told him everything, about the letters, the trip to the historical society, everything, finishing up with, "And the thing is, I didn't want you to know, because if your body really is buried out there, and they find it, well, that means that there's no reason for you to hang around here anymore, and I know it's selfish, but I would really miss you, so I was hoping if I didn't mention it you wouldn't find out and everything could just go on like normal."

But Jesse didn't have at all the sort of reaction to this information that I thought he would. He didn't sweep me into his arms and kiss me passionately like in the movies, or even call me *querida*, whatever it means, and stroke my hair, which was wet from my shower.

Instead, he just started laughing.

Which I didn't really appreciate. I mean, after everything I had gone through for him in the past twenty-four hours, you would think he would show a bit more gratitude than to sit there and laugh. Especially when my life might very well be in mortal peril.

I mentioned this to him, but that only made him laugh harder.

Finally, when he was through laughing—which didn't happen until I'd pulled the hammer out from under the covers, something that sent him into fresh peals, but what was I supposed to do? it was still digging into me—he did reach out and sort of ruffle my hair, but there wasn't anything the least bit romantic about it, since I had put Kiehl's leave-in conditioner on it, and I'm pretty sure it got on his fingers.

That just made me madder at him than ever, even though technically it wasn't his fault. So I took the ax out from beneath the sheets, too, and then pulled the covers up over my head and rolled over and wouldn't talk to him anymore. Or look at him. Very mature, I know, but I was peeved.

"Susannah," he said in a voice that was a little hoarse from all the laughing he'd been doing. I felt like punching him. I really did. "Don't be like that. I'm sorry. I'm sorry I laughed. It's just that I didn't understand a word you just said, you were talking so fast. And then when you pulled out that hammer—"

"Go away," I said.

"Come on, Susannah," Jesse said in his silkiest,

most persuasive voice—which he was using on purpose to make me go all squishy. Except that it wasn't going to work this time. "Let go of the sheet."

"No," I said, clutching the sheet tighter as he plucked at it. "I said go away."

"No, I won't go away. Sit up. I want to talk to you seriously now, but how can I do that when you won't look at me? Turn around."

"No," I said. I was really mad. I mean, you would have been, too. That Maria was one scary individual. And he'd been going to marry her! Well, a hundred and fifty years ago, anyway. Had he even *known* her? Known that she wasn't anything like the girl who'd written those idiotic letters to him? What had he been thinking, anyway?

"Why don't you just go hang out with Maria?" I suggested to him acidly. "Maybe you two could sit around and sharpen her knives together and have some more laughs at my expense. Ha ha, you could say. That mediator is so funny."

"Maria?" Jesse pulled on the sheet some more. "What are you talking about, knives?"

Okay. So I hadn't been totally up front with him. I hadn't told him the whole story. Yeah, the part about the letters and the historical society and the hole and all. But the part about Maria showing up with the knife—the reason, in fact, that I was sleeping in Doc's bed with a bunch of tools? Hadn't mentioned that part.

Because I'd known how he was going to react. Exactly the way he did.

"Maria and knives?" he echoed. "No. No."

That did it. I rolled over and said to him, very sarcastically, "Oh, okay, Jesse. So that knife she held to my throat last night, that must have been an *imaginary* knife. And I must have *imagined* it when she threatened to kill me, too."

I started to roll back over in a huff, but this time he caught me before I got turned all the way and swung me back around to face him. He wasn't, I saw with some satisfaction, laughing now. Or even smiling.

"A knife?" He was looking down at me like he wasn't sure he'd heard me right. "Maria was here? With a knife? Why?"

"You tell me," I said, even though I knew the answer perfectly well. "Someone's been dead and gone for as long as she has, it would have to take something pretty big to bring her back."

Jesse just stared down at me with those dark, liquid eyes of his. If he knew anything, he wasn't saying. Not just yet.

"She—she tried to hurt you?"

I nodded, and had the satisfaction of feeling his grip on my shoulders tighten.

"Yes," I said. "And she held it right here"—I pointed to my jugular—"and she said if I didn't tell Andy to stop digging, she was going to k—"

Kill me, was what I was going to say, but I didn't get a chance to, because Jesse snatched me up—really, snatched, that's the only way to describe it—and held on to me very tightly for someone who had thought the whole thing a big funny joke just a few seconds before.

This was, I must say, extremely gratifying. It got even more gratifying when Jesse said some stuff—though I didn't know what it was, because it was in Spanish—into my wet hair.

But that death grip (excuse the pun) he had me in didn't need any translating: He was scared. Scared for *me.*

"It was a really *large* knife," I said, enjoying the feel of his big strong shoulder beneath my cheek. I could totally get used to this. "And very pointy."

"Querida," he said. Okay, that word I understood. Well, sort of. He kissed the top of my head.

This was good. This was *very* good. I decided to go in for the kill.

"And then," I said, doing a very good imitation of sounding like I was crying, or at least, was pretty close to doing so, "she put her hand over my face to keep me from screaming, and one of her rings cut me and made my mouth all bloody."

Oops. This one did not have the desired effect. I should probably not have brought up my bloody mouth, since instead of kissing me there, which was what I'd been aiming for, he pulled me away from him so he could look down into my face.

"Susannah, why didn't you tell me any of this last night?" He looked genuinely baffled. "I asked you if something was wrong, and you never said a word."

Hello? Hadn't he heard anything I just said?

"Because." I was speaking through gritted teeth, but you would have, too, if the man of your dreams was holding you in his arms and all he wanted to do was talk. And about his ex-girlfriend's attempt to murder you, no less.

"It obviously has something to do with why you're here," I said. "Why you're still here, I mean, in this house, and why you've been here so long. Jesse, don't you see? If they find your body, that proves you were murdered, and that means Colonel Clemmings was right."

Jesse's bewilderment seemed to increase, rather than lessen, thanks to this explanation.

"Colonel who?" he said.

"Colonel Clemmings," I said. "Author of *My Monterey*. His theory of why you disappeared is not that you got cold feet about marrying Maria and went off to San Francisco to stake a claim, but that that Diego guy killed you so he could marry Maria himself. And if they find your body, Jesse, that will prove you were murdered. And the most likely suspects are, of course, Maria and that Diego dude."

But instead of being dazzled by my excellent sleuthing skills, Jesse asked in a shocked voice, "How do you know about him? About Diego?"

"I told you." God, this was irritating. When were we going to get to the kissing? "It's from a book Doc got out of the library. *My Monterey*, by Colonel Harold Clemmings."

"But Doc—I mean, David—is at camp, I thought."

I said frustratedly, "This was a long time ago. When I first got here. Last January."

Jesse didn't let go of me or anything, but he had an extremely odd look on his face.

"Are you saying that you've known about this . . . how I died . . . all along?"

"Yes," I said, a little defensively. I was getting the feeling that maybe he thought I'd done something wrong, prying into his death. "But, Jesse, that's my job. That's what mediators *do*. I can't help it."

"Why did you keep asking me about how I died, then," he demanded, "if you already knew?"

I said, still on the defensive side, "Well, I didn't know. Not for sure. I still don't. But Jesse—" I wanted to make sure he understood this part, so I pulled back (and he unfortunately let go of me, but what could I do?) and sat up on my heels and said, very slowly and carefully, "If they find your body out there, not only is Maria going to be really mad, but you . . . you're going to move on. You know? From here. Because that's what's been holding you back, Jesse. The mystery of what happened to you. Once your body is found, though, that mystery will be solved. And you'll go. And that's why I couldn't tell you, you see? Because I don't want you to go. Because I l—"

Oh my God, I almost said it. I can't even tell you how close I came to saying it. I got out the L and then the O just seemed to follow.

But at the last minute I was able to save it. I turned it to "—*like* having you around and I would really hate not seeing you anymore."

Swift, huh? That was a close one.

Because one thing I know for sure about guys, along with their inability to use a glass and lower the toilet seat and refill ice trays once they are empty: They really cannot handle the L word. I mean, it says so in just about every article I've ever read.

And you have to figure this is true of all guys, even guys who were born a hundred and fifty years ago.

And I guess my not using the L word paid off, since Jesse reached out and touched my cheek with his fingertips—just like he had done that day in the hospital.

"Susannah," he said. "Finding my body is not going to change anything."

"Um," I said. "Excuse me, Jesse, but I think I know what I'm talking about. I've been a mediator for sixteen years."

"Susannah," he said. "I have been dead for a hundred and fifty years. I think I know what *I* am talking about. And I can assure you, this mystery about my death you speak of . . . that is not why I, as you put it, am hanging around here."

A funny thing happened then. Just like in Clive Clemmings's office, earlier that day, I just started crying. Really. Just like that.

Oh, I wasn't sobbing like a baby or anything, but my eyes filled up with tears and I got that bad prickly feeling behind my nose, and my throat started to hurt. It was weird, because I'd just, you know, been trying to *act* as if I were crying, and then all of a sudden, I really was.

"Jesse," I said in this horrible sniffly kind of voice (acting like you're going to cry is way preferable to actually crying, as there is much less mucus involved), "I'm sorry, but that's just not possible. I mean, I *know*. I've done this a hundred times. When they find your body out there, that is it. You're gone."

"Susannah," he said again. And this time he didn't just touch my cheek. He reached up and cupped the side of my face with one hand . . .

Although the romantic effect was somewhat ruined by the fact that he was half laughing at me. To give him credit, though, he looked as if he were trying just as hard not to laugh as I was trying not to cry.

"I promise you, Susannah," he said with a lot of pauses between the words to give them emphasis, "that I am not going anywhere, whether or not your stepfather finds my body in the backyard. All right?"

I didn't believe him, of course. I wanted to and all, but the truth is, he didn't know what he was talking about.

What could I do, though? I had no choice but

to be brave about it. I mean, I couldn't very well just sit there and cry my eyes out over it. What kind of fool would I seem then?

So I said, unfortunately in a very mucusy manner, since by that time the tears were sort of spilling out, "Really? You promise?"

Jesse grinned and let go of my face. Then he reached into his pocket and pulled out a small, lace-trimmed thing I recognized. Maria de Silva's handkerchief. He'd used it before to bind up various cuts and scrapes I'd sustained in the line of mediation duty. Now he used it to wipe my tears.

"I swear," he said, laughing. But just a little.

In the end, he persuaded me to come back to my own bed. He said he'd make sure his ex-girlfriend didn't come after me in the night. Only he didn't call her his ex-girlfriend. He just called her Maria. I still wanted to ask him what he'd been thinking, going out with a ferret-faced ice bitch like her, but there never really seemed to be a right moment.

Is there ever a right moment to ask someone why they were going to marry the person who had had them killed?

Probably not.

I don't know how Jesse thought he was going to stop Maria if she came back. True, he had been dead a lot longer than she had, so he had had a little more practice at the whole ghost thing. It seemed pretty likely, in fact, that Maria's haunting of me was her first and only visit back to this world from whatever spiritual plane she'd inhabited since her death. The longer someone has been a ghost, the more powerful they tend to be.

Unless, of course, like Maria, they happened to be filled with rage.

But Jesse and I had, together, fought ghosts every bit as angry as Maria, and won. We would win this time, too, I knew, so long as we stuck together.

It was definitely strange going to bed knowing someone was going to be sitting there, watching me sleep. But after I got used to the idea, it was sort of nice, knowing he was there with Spike on the daybed, reading a book called *A Thousand Years* he'd found in Doc's room, by the light of his own spectral glow. It would have been more romantic if he'd just sat there gazing longingly at my face, but beggars can't be choosers, and how many other girls do you know who have boys perfectly willing to sit in their bedrooms and watch for evil trespassers all night? I bet you can't even name one.

I suppose eventually I must have fallen asleep,

since when I opened my eyes again it was morning, and Jesse was still there. He had finished *A Thousand Years* and had moved on to a book from one of my shelves called *Bridges of Madison County*, which he seemed to find excruciatingly amusing, although he was trying not to laugh loud enough to wake me.

God, how embarrassing.

I didn't realize then that it was the last time I'd ever see him.

chapter *seven*

My day pretty much went downhill from there.

I guess while Maria wasn't that interested in renewing her acquaintance with her ex, she was still plenty interested in torturing me. I got my first inkling of this when I opened the refrigerator and pulled out the brand-new carton of orange juice someone had bought to replace the one finished off by Dopey and Sleepy the day before.

I had just opened it when Dopey stomped in, snatched the carton from me, and lifted it to his lips.

I started to go, "Hey!" in an irritated voice, but the word soon turned into a shriek of disgust and terror when what poured into my stepbrother's mouth was not juice, but bugs.

Hundreds of bugs. Thousands of bugs. *Live* bugs, wriggling and crawling and falling from his open mouth.

Dopey realized what was happening about a split second after I did. He threw the carton down and ran to the sink, spitting out as many of the black beetles that had fallen into his mouth as he could. Meanwhile, they were still swarming over the sides of the carton onto the floor.

I don't know how I summoned the inner strength to do what I did next. If there's one thing I hate, it's bugs. Next to poison oak, it is one of the main reasons I spend so little time in the great outdoors. I mean, I do not mind the odd ant drowning in a pool or a butterfly landing on my shoulder, but show me a mosquito or, God forbid, a cockroach, and I am out the door.

Still, despite my near crippling fear of anything smaller than a peanut, I picked up that carton and poured its contents down the sink, then, quicker than you can say Raid, flicked on the disposal.

"Ohmygawd!" Dopey was yelling, as he continued to spit into the sink. "Ohmyfreakingawd."

Only he didn't say freaking. Under the circumstances, I didn't blame him.

Our shrieking had brought Sleepy and my stepfather into the kitchen. They just stood there staring at the hundreds of black beetles that had escaped death by the kitchen drain and were scurrying around the terra-cotta tiles. At least until I yelled, "Step on them!"

Then we all started stomping on as many of the disgusting things as we could.

When we were through, only a couple ended up getting away, the ones that had the sense to make for the crack beneath the fridge, and one or two that made it all the way to the open sliding glass doors to the deck. It had been arduous, disgusting work, and we all stood around panting . . . except for Dopey, who, with a groan, rushed off into the bathroom, presumably to rinse with Listerine, or maybe to check for any antennas that might have gotten caught between his teeth.

"Well," Andy said, when I explained what had happened. "That's the last time I buy organic."

Which was kind of funny, in a sick way. Except that I happened to know that organic or frozen from concentrate, it wouldn't have made any difference: A poltergeist had been at work.

Andy looked at the mess on the floor and said in a sort of dazed voice, "We have to get this cleaned up before your mother gets home."

He had that right. You think I've got a thing about bugs? You should see my mother. We are neither of us what you would call nature lovers.

We threw ourselves into our work, scrubbing and scouring bug guts off the tile, while I made subtle suggestions that we order in for all our meals, not just supper, for the time being. I wasn't sure if Maria had gotten her hands on any other foodstuffs, but I suspected nothing in the pantry or refrigerator was going to be safe.

Andy was only too willing to go along with this, blathering on about how insect infestations can destroy entire crops, and how many homes he'd worked on had been destroyed by termites, and how important it was to have your house regularly fumigated.

But fumigation, I wanted to say to him, doesn't do any good when the bugs are the result of a vengeful ghost.

But, of course, I didn't mention this. I highly doubt he would have understood what I was talking about. Andy doesn't believe in ghosts.

Must be nice to have that luxury.

When Sleepy and I finally got to work, it appeared briefly that things were looking up, since we did not even get in trouble for being late. This was, of course, on account of Sleepy having

Caitlin so firmly in his thrall. So you see, there are *some* advantages to having stepbrothers.

There did not even seem to have been a complaint from the Slaters about my having taken Jack off hotel property without their permission, since I was told to go straight to their suite. This, I thought to myself as I made my way down the thickly carpeted hotel corridors to their rooms, really is too good to be true, and just goes to show that behind every cloud is a slice of clear blue sky.

At least, that's what I was thinking as I knocked on their door. When it swung open, however, to reveal not just Jack, but both Slater brothers dressed in swimwear, I began to have my doubts.

Jack pounced on me like a kitten on a ball of yarn.

"Guess what?" he cried. "Paul's not playing golf or tennis or anything today. He wants to spend the whole day with *us*. Isn't that great?"

"Um," I said.

"Yeah, Suze," Paul said. He had on long baggy swim trunks (proving that it could have been worse: He could have been wearing one of those micro Speedos) and a towel wrapped around his neck and nothing else, except a smirk. "Isn't that great?"

"Um," I said. "Yeah. Great."

Dr. and Mrs. Slater scooted past us in their golf clothes. "You kids have fun now," Nancy called. "Suze, we've got lessons all day. You'll stay until five, won't you?" Then, without waiting for an answer, she said, "Okay, buh-bye," took her husband by the arm, and left.

Okay, I said to myself. *I can handle this.* Already that morning I'd handled a swarm of bugs. I mean, despite the fact that every once in a while I thought I felt one crawling on me and jumped, only to find it was just my own hair or whatever, I had recovered pretty well. Far better, probably, than Dopey ever would.

So I could certainly handle having Paul Slater around all day bugging me. Um, I mean bothering me.

Right? No problem.

Except that it *was* a problem. Because Jack kept wanting to talk about the whole mediator thing, and I kept muttering for him to shut up, and then he'd go, "Oh, it's okay, Suze, Paul knows."

Which was the point. Paul wasn't *supposed* to know. It was supposed to be our secret, mine and Jack's. I didn't want stupid, nonbelieving, since-you-won't-go-out-with-me-I'm-telling-on-you Paul to have any part of it. Especially since every time Jack mentioned anything about it, Paul lowered his Armanis and looked at me over the top of the frames, all expectantly, waiting to hear what I'd say.

What could I do? I pretended I didn't know what Jack was talking about. Which was frustrating to him, of course, but what else was I supposed to do? I didn't want Paul knowing my business. I mean, my own mother doesn't know. Why on earth would I tell *Paul*?

Fortunately, after the first six or seven times Jack tried to mention anything mediator-related and I ignored him, he seemed to get the message and shut up. It helped that the pool had gotten very crowded with other little kids and their parents and sitters, so he had plenty to distract him.

But it was still a little unnerving, leaning there against the side of the pool with Kim, who'd shown up with her charges, to glance at Paul every so often and see him stretched out on a deck chair, his face turned in my direction. Especially since I had the feeling that Paul, unlike Sleepy, up in his chair, was wide awake behind the dark lenses of his sunglasses.

Then again, as Kim put it, "Hey, if a hottie like that wants to look at me, he can look all he wants."

But of course, it's different for Kim. She doesn't have the ghost of a hundred-and-fifty-year-old hottie living in her bedroom.

All in all, I would say the morning turned out pretty wretchedly, considering. I figured that, after lunch, the day could only get better.

Was I ever wrong. After lunch was when the cops showed up.

I was stretched out on a lounge chair of my own, keeping one eye on Jack, who was playing a pretty rambunctious game of Marco Polo with Kim's kids, and another on Paul, who was pretending to read a copy of *The Nation*, but who was, as Kim pointed out, spying on us over the top of the pages, when Caitlin appeared, looking visibly upset, followed by two burly members of the Carmel police.

I assumed that they were merely passing through, on the way to the men's locker room, where there'd been an occasional break-in. Imagine my great surprise when Caitlin led the cops right up to me and said in a shaking voice, "This is Susannah Simon, Officers."

I hurried to climb into my hideous khaki shorts, while Kim, in the lounge chair beside mine, gaped up at the cops like they were mermen risen from the sea or something.

"Miss Simon," the taller of the cops said. "We'd just like a word with you for a moment, if you don't mind."

I've talked to more than my fair share of cops in my time. Not because I hang out with gang-bangers, as Sleepy likes to think, but because in mediating, one often is forced to, well, bend the law a little.

For instance, let's say Marisol had not turned that rosary over to Jorge's daughter. Well, in order to carry out Jorge's last wishes, I would have been forced to break into Marisol's home, take the rosary myself, and mail it to Teresa anonymously. Anyone can see how something like that, which is really for the greater good in the vast scheme of things, might be misinterpreted by local law enforcement as a crime.

So, yes, the fact of the matter is, I have been hauled before the cops any number of times, much to my poor mother's chagrin. However, with the exception of that unfortunate incident that had landed me in the hospital some months prior, I had not done anything lately, that I could think of, that could even remotely be construed as unlawful.

So it was with some curiosity, but little trepidation, that I followed the officers—Knightley and

Jones—out of the pool area and behind the Pool House Grill, near the Dumpsters, the closest area where, I suppose, the officers felt we could be assured total privacy for our little chat.

"Miss Simon," Officer Knightley, the taller policeman, began, as I watched a lizard dart out of the shade of a nearby rhododendron, look at us in alarm, and then dart back into the shadows. "Are you acquainted with a Dr. Clive Clemmings?"

I was shocked into admitting that I was. The last thing I had expected Officer Knightley to mention was Dr. Clive Clemmings, Ph.D. I was thinking something more along the lines of, oh, I don't know. Taking an eight-year-old off hotel property without his parents' permission.

Stupid, I know, but Paul had really rattled me with that one.

"Why?" I asked. "Is he—Mr. Clemmings—all right?"

"Unfortunately, no," Officer Jones said. "He's dead."

"Dead?" I wanted to reach out for something to hold on to. Unfortunately there wasn't anything to grab except the Dumpster, and since it was filled with the remains of that afternoon's lunch, I didn't want to touch it.

I settled for sinking down onto the curb.

Clive Clemmings? My mind was racing. Clive Clemmings *dead*? How? *Why*? I hadn't liked Clive Clemmings, of course. I'd been hoping that when Jesse's body turned up, I could go back to his office and rub it in his face. You know, the whole part about Jesse having been murdered after all.

Only now it looked as if I wouldn't get the chance.

"What happened?" I asked, gazing up at the cops bewilderedly.

"We're not sure, precisely," Officer Knightley said. "He was found this morning at his desk at the historical society, dead from an apparent heart attack. According to the receptionist's sign-in log, you were one of the few people who saw him yesterday."

Only then did I remember that the lady behind the reception desk had made me sign in. Damn!

"Well," I said heartily—but not too heartily, I hoped. "He was fine when I talked to him."

"Yes," Officer Knightley said. "We're aware of that. It's not Dr. Clemmings's death we're here about."

"It isn't?" *Wait a minute. What was going on?*

"Miss Simon," Officer Jones said. "When Dr. Clemmings was found this morning, it was also discovered than an item of particular value to the historical society was missing. Something you apparently looked at, with Dr. Clemmings, just yesterday."

The letters. Maria's letters. They were gone. They had to be. She had come and taken them, and Clive Clemmings had caught a glimpse of her somehow and had had a heart attack from the shock of seeing the woman in the portrait behind his desk walking around his office.

"A small painting." Officer Knightley had to refer to his notepad. "A miniature of someone named Hector de Silva. The receptionist, Mrs. Lampbert, says Dr. Clemmings told her you were particularly interested in it."

This information, so unexpected, shook me. Jesse's *portrait*? Jesse's portrait was gone from the collection? But who would have taken *that*? And *why*?

I did not have to feign my innocence for once as I stammered, "I—I looked at the painting, yes. But I didn't take it or anything. I mean, when I left, Mr.—Dr. Clemmings was putting it away."

Officers Knightley and Jones exchanged glances. Before they could say anything more, however, someone came around the corner of the Pool House.

It was Paul Slater.

"Is there a problem with my brother's baby-sitter, officers?" he demanded in a bored voice that suggested—to me, anyway—that the Slater family's employees were often being dragged off for questioning by members of law enforcement.

"Excuse me," Officer Knightley said, sounding really very offended. "But as soon as we are done questioning this witness, we—"

Paul whipped off his sunglasses and barked, "Are you aware that Miss Simon is a minor? Shouldn't you be questioning her in the presence of her parents?"

Officer Jones blinked a few times. "Pardon me, uh, sir," he began, though it was clear he didn't really consider Paul a sir, seeing as how he was under eighteen and all. "The young lady isn't under arrest. We're just asking her a few—"

"If she isn't under arrest," Paul said swiftly, "then she doesn't have to speak to you at all, does she?"

Officers Knightley and Jones looked at each other again. Then Officer Knightley said, "Well, no. But there has been a death and a theft, and we have reason to believe she might have information—"

Paul looked at me. "Suze," he said, "have these gentlemen read you your rights?"

"Um," I said. "No."

"Do you want to talk to them?"

"Um," I said, glancing nervously from Officer Knightley to Officer Jones, and then back again. "Not really."

"Then you don't have to."

Paul leaned down and took hold of my arm.

"Say good-bye to the nice police officers," he said, pulling me to my feet.

I looked up at the police officers. "Uh," I said to them. "I'm very sorry Dr. Clemmings is dead, but I swear I don't know what happened to him, or that painting, either. Bye."

Then I let Paul Slater pull me back out to the pool.

I am not normally so docile, but I have to tell you, I was in shock. Maybe it was post-being-questioned-by-the-police-but-not-taken-down-to-the-station-house exhilaration, but once we were out of the sight of Officers Knightley and Jones, I whirled around and grabbed Paul's wrist.

"All right," I said. "What was all that about?"

Paul had put his sunglasses back on, so it was hard to read the expression in his eyes, but I think he was amused.

"All what?" he asked.

"All that," I said, nodding toward the back of

the Pool House. "That whole Lone-Ranger-to-the-rescue thing. Correct me if I'm wrong, but wasn't it just yesterday that you were going to turn me over to the authorities yourself? Or rat me out to my boss, anyway?"

Paul shrugged. "Yes," he said. "A certain someone pointed out to me, however, that you catch more flies with honey than you do with vinegar."

At the time, all I felt was a little miffed at being called a fly. It didn't even occur to me to wonder who that "certain someone" might have been.

It wasn't long before I found out, however.

chapter *eight*

Okay, so I went out with him.

So what?

So what does that make me? I mean, the guy asked me if I wanted to go with him for a burger after I dumped his brother back off with his parents at five, and I said yes.

Why shouldn't I have said yes? What did I have to look forward to at home, huh? Certainly not any hope of dinner. Roach à la mode? Spider fricassee?

Oh, yeah, and a ghost who had her fiancé murdered and was going to try to off me next, at her earliest opportunity.

I thought maybe I'd misjudged Paul. Maybe I hadn't been fair. I mean, yeah, he had been kind of stalkerish the day before, but he more than made up for it with the whole rescuing-me-from-the-police thing.

And he didn't make a single move on me. Not one. When I said I wanted to go home, he said no problem, and took me home.

It certainly wasn't his fault that when we drove up to my house, he couldn't pull into the driveway on account of all the police cars and ambulances parked there.

I swear, one thing I am getting with my summer job money is a cell phone. Because stuff keeps on happening, and I have no idea, because I'm off having burgers with someone at Friday's.

I jumped out of the car and ran up to where I saw all the people standing. When I reached the caution tape, which was strung up all around the hole where the hot tub was supposed to go, someone grabbed me by the waist and spun me around before I had a chance to do what I intended, which was, although I'm not too clear on this, scramble down into the hole, to join the people I saw down at the bottom of it, bending over something that I was pretty sure was a body.

But, like I said, someone stopped me.

"Whoa, tiger," that someone said, swinging me around. It turned out to be Andy, looking extremely dirty and sweaty and unlike his normal self. "Hang on. Nothing for you to see there."

"Andy." The sun hadn't quite set, but I was having trouble seeing anyway. It was like I was in a tunnel, and all I could see was this bright pinprick of light at the end of it. "Andy, where's my mom?"

"Your mom's fine," Andy said. "Everyone's fine."

The pinprick started getting a little wider. I could see my mom's face now, peering at me worriedly from the deck, with Dopey behind her, wearing his usual sneer.

"Then what—" I saw the men in the bottom of the hole lift up a stretcher. On the stretcher was a black body bag like the kind you always see on TV. "Who is that?" I wanted to know.

"Well, we're not sure," my stepfather said. "But whoever he is, he's been there a very long time, so chances are, he isn't anyone we know."

Dopey's face loomed large in my line of vision.

"It's a skeleton," he informed me with a good deal of relish. He appeared to have gotten over the fact that only that morning he'd had a mouth full of beetles, and was back to his normal insufferable self. "It was totally awesome, Suze, you should have been here. My shovel went right through his skull. It cracked like it was an egg or something."

Well, that was enough for me. My tunnel vision came right back, but not soon enough to miss something that tumbled from the stretcher as it went past me. My gaze locked on it and followed it as it fluttered to the ground, landing very near my feet. It was only a deeply stained and extremely threadbare piece of material, no bigger than my hand. A rag, it looked like, though you could see that at one time it had had lace around its edges. Little bits of lace still clung to it like burrs, especially around the corner where, very faintly, you could read three embroidered initials:

MDS.

Maria de Silva. It was the handkerchief Jesse had used last night to dry my tears. Only it was the real handkerchief, frayed and brown with age.

And it had fallen out of the jumble of decaying material holding Jesse's bones together.

I turned around and threw up my Friday's bacon cheeseburger and potato skins all over the side of the house.

Needless to say, no one except my mother was very sympathetic about this. Dopey declared it the most disgusting thing he had ever seen.

Apparently he'd forgotten what he'd had in his mouth less then twelve hours before. Andy simply went and got the hose, and Sleepy, equally unimpressed, said he had to get going or he'd be late delivering 'za.

My mother insisted on putting me to bed, even though having her in my room just then was about the last thing I wanted. I mean, I had just seen them removing Jesse's body from my backyard. I would have liked to have discussed this disturbing sight with him, but how could I do that with my mother there?

I figured if I just let her fuss over me for half an hour, she'd go. But she stayed much longer than that, making me take a shower and change out of my uniform and into a silky pair of lounging pajamas she'd bought me for Valentine's Day (pathetically, it was the only Valentine I received). Then she insisted on combing my hair out, like she used to when I was a little kid.

She wanted to talk, too, of course. She had plenty to say on the subject of the skeleton Andy and Dopey had found, insisting it was only "some poor man" who had gotten killed in a shoot-out back in the days when our home was a boarding-house for mercenaries and gunslingers and the odd rancher's son. She said the police would insist on treating it as a homicide until the coroner had determined how long the body had been there, but since, she went on, the fellow still had his spurs on (spurs!) she assumed they would come to the same conclusion she had: that this guy had been dead for a lot longer than any of us had been alive.

She tried to make me feel better. But how could she? She didn't have any idea why I was so upset. I mean, I'm not Jack. I had never blabbed to her about my secret talent. My mom didn't know that I knew whose skeleton that was. She didn't know that just twelve hours ago he had been sitting on my daybed, laughing at *Bridges of Madison County*. And that a few hours before that, he had kissed me—albeit on the top of my head, but still.

I mean, come on. You'd be upset, too.

Finally, finally she left. I heaved a sigh of relief, thinking I could relax, you know?

But no. Oh, no. Because my mother didn't retreat with the intention of leaving me alone. I found that out the hard way a couple of minutes later when the phone rang, and Andy hollered up the stairs that it was for me. I really did not feel like talking to anyone, but what could I do? Andy had already said I was home. So I picked up, and whose cheerful little voice do I hear on the other end?

That's right.

Doc's.

"Suze, how are you doing?" my youngest step-brother wanted to know. Although clearly he already knew. How I was doing, I mean. Obviously, my mother had called him at camp—who gets calls from their stepmother at *camp*, I ask you?—and told him to call me. Because, of course, she knows. She knows he's the only one of my stepbrothers I can stand, and I'm sure she thought I might tell him whatever it was that was bothering me, and then she could pump him for information later.

My mother isn't an award-winning television news journalist for nothing, you know.

"Suze?" Doc sounded concerned. "Your mom told me about . . . what happened. Do you want me to come home?"

I flopped back down on my pillows. "Home? No, I don't want you to come home. Why would I want you to come home?"

"Well," Doc said. He lowered his voice as if he suspected someone was listening in. "Because of Jesse."

Out of all the people I live with, Doc was the

only one who had the slightest idea that We Are Not Alone. Doc believed . . . and he had good reason to. Once when I'd been in a real jam, Jesse had gone to him. Scared out of his wits, Doc had nevertheless come through for me.

And now he was offering to do so again.

Only what could he do? Nothing. Worse than nothing, he could actually get hurt. I mean, look at what had happened to Dopey that morning. Did I want to see Doc with a faceful of bugs? No way.

"No," I said quickly. "No, Doc—I mean, David. That isn't necessary. You stay where you are. Things are fine here. Really."

Doc sounded disappointed. "Suze, things are *not* fine. Do you want to talk about it, at least?"

Oh, yeah. I want to discuss my love life—or lack thereof—with my twelve-year-old stepbrother.

"Not really," I said.

"Look, Suze," Doc said. "I know it had to be upsetting. I mean, seeing his skeleton like that. But you've got to remember that our bodies are simply the vessel—and a very crude one, at that—in which our souls are carried while we're alive on earth. Jesse's body . . . well, it doesn't have anything to do with him anymore."

Easy for him to say, I thought miserably. He'd

never gotten a look at Jesse's abs.

Not that, if he had, they would have interested Doc much, of course.

"Really," Doc went on, "if you think about it, that's probably not the only body Jesse's going to have. According to the Hindus, we shed our outer shells—our bodies—several times. In fact, we keep doing so, depending on our karma, until we finally get it right, thus achieving liberation from the cycle of rebirth."

"Oh?" I stared at the canopy over my bed. I really could not believe I was having this conversation. And with a twelve-year-old. "Do we?"

"Sure. Most of us, anyway. I mean, unless we get it right the first time. But that hardly ever happens. See, what's going on with Jesse is that his karma is all messed up, and he got bumped off the path to nirvana. He just needs to find his way back into the body he's supposed to get after, you know, his last one, and then he'll be fine."

"David," I said. "Are you sure you're at computer camp? Because it sounds to me like maybe Mom and Andy dropped you off at yoga camp by mistake."

"Suze," Doc said with a sigh. "Look. All I'm saying is, that skeleton you saw, it wasn't Jesse, all right? It has nothing to do with him anymore.

So don't let it upset you. Okay?"

I decided it was high time to change the subject.

"So," I said. "Any cute girls at that camp?"

"Suze," he said severely. "Don't—"

"I knew it," I said. "What's her name?"

"Shut up," Doc said. "Look, I gotta go. But remember what I said, will you? I'll be home Sunday, so we can talk more then."

"Fine," I said. "See you then."

"See you. And Suze?"

"Yeah, Doc—I mean, David?"

"Be careful, okay? That Diego—the guy from that book, who supposedly killed Jesse?—he seemed kind of . . . mean. You might want to watch your back or . . . well, whatever."

Whatever was right.

But I didn't say so to Doc. Instead, I said goodbye. What else could I say? Felix Diego isn't the half of it, sonny? I was too upset even to entertain the idea that I might possibly have a second hostile spirit to deal with.

But I didn't even know what upset was until Spike came scrambling through my open window, looked around expectantly, and meowed. . . .

And Jesse didn't show up.

Not even after I called out his name.

They don't, as a rule. Ghosts, I mean. Come

142

when you call them.

But for the most part, Jesse does. Although lately he's been showing up before I even had a chance to call him, when I've only *thought* about calling him. Then *wham*, next thing I knew, there he was.

Except not this time.

Nothing. Not a flicker.

Well, I said to myself as I fed Spike his can of food and tried to remain calm, *that's okay*. I mean, it doesn't mean anything. Maybe he's busy. I mean, that was his skeleton down there. Maybe he's following it to wherever they're taking it. To the morgue or whatever. It's probably very traumatic, watching people dig up your body. Jesse didn't know anything about Hinduism and karma. At least, that I knew of. To him, his body had probably been a lot more than just a vessel for his soul.

That's where he was. The morgue. Watching what they did with his remains.

But when the hours passed, and it got dark out, and Spike, who usually goes out prowling at night for small vermin and any Chihuahuas he can find, actually climbed onto my bed, where I sat leafing sightlessly through magazines, and butted his head against my hand . . .

Well, that's when I knew.

That's when I knew something was really, really wrong. Because that cat hates my guts, even though I'm the one who feeds him. If he's climbing up onto my bed and butting his head against my hand, well, I'm sorry, that means the universe as I know it is crumbling.

Because Jesse isn't coming back.

Except, I kept telling myself as my panic mounted, *he promised*. He *swore*.

But as the minutes ticked past and there was still no sign of him, I knew. I just knew. He was gone. They'd found his body, and that meant he was no longer missing, and that meant there was no need for him to hang around my room. Not anymore, just like I'd tried to explain to him last night.

Only he had sounded so sure . . . so sure that that wasn't it. He had laughed. He had *laughed* when I first said it, like it was ridiculous.

But then where was he? If he wasn't gone—to heaven, or to his next life (not to hell; there's no place, I'm sure, for Jesse in hell, if there is a hell)—then *where was he*?

I tried calling my dad. Not on the phone or anything because, of course, my dad can't be reached that way, being dead. I tried calling to him wherever he was, out there on the astral plane.

Only of course he didn't come, either. But then, he never does. Well, sometimes he does. But rarely, and not this time.

I just want you to know that I don't normally freak out like this. I mean, normally, I am very much a woman of action. Something happens and, well, I go kick some butts. That's how it usually works.

But this . . .

For some reason, I couldn't think straight. I really couldn't. I was just sitting there in my hunter green lounging pajamas, going, *What should I do? What should I do?*

Seriously. It was not good.

Which was why I did what I did next. If I couldn't figure out what to do myself, well, I needed someone to tell me what to do. And I knew just the someone who could.

I had to talk quietly because, of course, by that time it was past eleven, and everyone in the house but me was asleep.

"Is Father Dominic there?" I asked.

The person on the other end of the phone—an older man, from the sound of it—went, "What's that, honey? I can barely hear you."

"Father Dominic," I said, speaking as loudly as I dared. "Please, I need to speak to Father

Dominic right away. Is he there?"

"Sure, honey," the man on the phone said. Then I heard him yell, "Dom! Hey, Dom! Phone for you!"

Dom? How *dare* that man call Father Dominic *Dom?* Talk about disrespectful.

But all my indignation melted when I heard Father Dominic's soft, deep voice. I hadn't realized how much I'd missed him, not seeing him every day over the summer like I do during the school year. "Hello?"

"Father Dom," I said. No, I didn't say it. I'll admit it: I wept it. I was a basket case.

"Susannah?" Father Dominic sounded shocked. "What's wrong? Why are you crying? Are you all right?"

"Yes," I said. All right, not said: sobbed. "It's not me. It's J-Jesse."

"Jesse?" Father Dom's voice took on the note it always did when the subject of Jesse came up. It'd taken him a while to warm up to Jesse. I guess I could see why. Father D. is not only a priest, he's also the principal of a Catholic school. He's not supposed to approve of stuff like girls and guys sharing a bedroom . . . even if the guy is, you know, dead.

And I could understand it, because it's different

with mediators than it is with everyone else. Everyone else just walks through ghosts. They do it all the time, and they don't even know it. Oh, maybe they feel a cold spot, or they think they've glimpsed something out of the corner of their eye, but when they turn around, no one is there.

It's different for mediators. For us, ghosts are made up of matter, not shrouds of mist. I can't put my hand through Jesse, though anyone else could. Well, anyone else but Jack and Father Dom.

So it's understandable why Father Dom's never been too wild about Jesse, even though the guy's saved my life more times than I can count. Because whatever else he is, Jesse's still a guy, and he's living in my bedroom, and . . . well, you get the picture.

Not, of course, that there'd been anything going on—much to my chagrin.

The thing was, now there never would be. I mean, now I'd never even know if something *could* have happened. Because he was gone.

I didn't mention any of this to Father Dom, of course. I just told him what had happened, about Maria and the knife and the bugs, and about Clive Clemmings being dead and the missing portrait, and how they'd found Jesse's body and now he was gone.

"And he promised me," I finished, somewhat incoherently, because I was crying so hard. "He *swore* that wasn't it, that that wasn't what was holding him here. But now he's gone, and—"

Father Dominic's voice was soothing and controlled in comparison to my hiccupy ramblings.

"All right, Susannah," he said. "I understand. I understand. Obviously there are forces at work here that are beyond Jesse's control and, well, beyond yours, too, I might add. I'm glad you called me. You were right to call me. Listen, now, and do exactly as I say."

I sniffled. It felt so good—I can't even describe to you how good it felt—to have someone telling me what to do. Really. Ordinarily the last thing I want is to be told what to do. But in this case, I really, really appreciated it. I clung to the phone, waiting breathlessly for Father Dominic's instructions.

"You're in your room, I suppose?" Father D. said.

I nodded, realized he couldn't see me, and said, "Yes."

"Good. Wake your family and tell them exactly what you just told me. Then get out of the house. Get out of that house, Susannah, just as quickly as you can."

I took the phone away from my ear and looked at the receiver as if it had just started bleating in my ear like a sheep. Seriously. Because that would have made about as much sense as what Father Dom just said.

I put the receiver back to my ear.

"Susannah?" Father Dom was saying. "Did you hear me? I am perfectly serious about this. One man is already dead. I do not doubt that someone in your family will be next if you do not get them out of there."

I know I was a wreck and all. But I wasn't *that* much of a wreck.

"Father D.," I said. "I can't *tell* them—"

"Yes, you can, Susannah," Father Dominic said. "I always thought it was wrong of you to keep your gift a secret from your mother all these years. It's time you told her."

"As if," I said into the phone.

"Susannah," Father D. said. "The insects were only the beginning. If this de Silva woman is taking demonic possession of your household, horrors such as . . . well, horrors such as you or I could never even imagine are going to begin—"

"Demonic possession of my household?" I gripped the phone tighter. "Listen, Father D., she may have got my boyfriend, but she is *not* getting my house."

Father Dominic sounded tired. "Susannah," he

said. "Please, just do as I say. Get yourself and your family out of there, before harm comes to any of you. I understand that you are upset about Jesse, but the fact is, Susannah, that he is dead and you, at least for the time being, are still alive. We've got to do whatever we can to see that you remain that way. I will leave here now, but I'm a six-hour drive away. I promise I will be there in the morning. A thorough administration of holy water should drive away any evil spirits remaining in the house, but—"

Spike had padded across the room toward me. I thought he was going to bite me, as usual, but he didn't. Instead, he trotted right up to my face and let out a very loud, very plaintive cry.

"Good God," Father Dominic cried into the phone. "Is that her? Is she there already?"

I reached out and scratched Spike behind his one remaining ear, amazed he was even letting me touch him. "No," I said. "That was Spike. He misses Jesse."

Father Dominic said, "Susannah, I know how painful this must be for you. But you must know that wherever Jesse is now, he's better off than he's been for the past hundred and fifty years, living in limbo between this world and the next. I know it's difficult, but you must try to be happy for him, and know that, above all, he would want you to take care of yourself, Susannah. He would want you to keep yourself and your family safe—"

As I listened to Father Dom, I realized he was right. That *was* what Jesse would have wanted. And there I was, sitting around in a pair of lounging pajamas when there was work to be done.

"Father D.," I said, interrupting him. "In the cemetery, over at the Mission. Are there any de Silvas buried there?"

Father Dominic, startled from his safety-first lecture, said, "I—de Silva? Really, Susannah, I don't know. I don't think—"

"Oh, wait," I said. "I keep forgetting, she married a Diego. There's a Diego crypt, isn't there?" I tried to picture the cemetery, which was a small one, surrounded by high walls, directly behind the basilica down at the Mission where Father Dominic works and I go to school. There are only a small number of graves there, mainly of the monks who had first worked with Junipero Serra, the guy who'd founded the Carmel Mission back in the 1700s.

But a few wealthy landowners in the 1800s had managed to get a mausoleum or two squeezed in by donating a sizable portion of their fortunes to the church.

And the biggest one—if I remembered correctly from the time Mr. Walden, our world civ
teacher, had taken us to the cemetery to give us a
taste of our local history—had the word DIEGO
carved into the door.

"Susannah," Father Dominic said. For the first
time, there was a note of something other than
urgency in his voice. Now he sounded frightened.
"Susannah, I know what you are thinking, and I
. . . I forbid it! You are not to go near that cemetery, do you understand me? You are not to go
near that crypt! It is much too dangerous. . . ."

Just the way I like it.

But that's not what I said out loud. Aloud I
said, "Okay, Father D. You're right. I'll wake my
mom up. I'll tell her everything. And I'll get everyone out of the house."

Father Dominic was so astonished, he didn't
say anything for a minute. When he was finally
able to find his voice, he said, "Good. Well . . .
good, then. Yes. Get everyone out of the house.
Don't do anything foolish, Susannah, like call
upon the ghost of this woman, until I get there.
Promise me."

Promise me. Like promises mean anything
anymore. Look at Jesse. He'd promised me he
wasn't going to go away, and where was he?

Gone. Gone forever.

And I'd been too much of a coward ever to tell him how I really felt about him.

And now I'd never get the chance to.

"Sure," I said to Father Dominic. "I promise."

But I think even he knew I didn't mean it.

chapter *nine*

Ghost busting is a tricky business.

You'd think it would be easy, right? Like if a ghost's bothering you, you just, you know, bust its chops and it'll go away.

Yeah. Doesn't work that way much, unfortunately.

Which is not to say that busting someone's chops does not have therapeutic value. Especially for someone who, like me, might be grieving. Because that's what I was doing, of course. Grieving for Jesse.

Except—and I don't know if this applies to all mediators or just me—I don't really grieve like a normal person. I mean, I sat around and cried my eyes out after the realization first hit me that I was never going to see Jesse again.

But then something happened. I stopped feeling sad and started feeling mad.

Really mad. There I was, and it was after midnight, and I was extremely angry.

It wasn't that I didn't want to keep my promise to Father D. I really did. But I just couldn't.

Any more than Jesse could apparently keep his promise to me.

So it was only about fifteen minutes after my phone call to Father D. that I emerged from my bathroom—Jesse was gone, of course, so I could have changed in my room, but old habits die hard—in full ghost-busting regalia, including my tool belt and hooded sweatshirt, which even I will admit might seem a bit excessive for California in July. But it was nighttime, and that mist rolling in from the ocean in the wee hours can be chilly.

I don't want you to think I didn't give serious thought to what Father D. had said about my telling my mom everything and getting her and the Ackermans out of there. I really did think about it.

It's just that the more I thought about it, the more ridiculous it sounded. I mean, first of all, my mom is a television news journalist. She simply is not the type to believe in ghosts. She only believes in what she can see or, barring that, what has been proven to exist by science. The one time I did try to tell her, she totally did not understand. And I realized then that she never would.

So how could I possibly go busting into her bedroom and tell her and her new husband that they have to get out of the house because a vengeful spirit is after me? She would be on the phone to her therapist back in New York, looking for communities where I could go to "rest," so fast you wouldn't believe it.

So that plan was out.

But that was all right, because I had a much better one. One that, really, I should have thought of right away, but I guess that whole seeing-the-skeleton-of-the-guy-I-love-being-hauled-out-of-a-hole-in-my-backyard thing really got to me, and so I didn't think of it until I was on the phone with Father D.

But once I'd come up with it, I realized it really was the perfect plan. Instead of waiting for Maria to come to me, I was simply going to go to her and, well . . .

Send her back from where she came.

Or reduce her to a mound of quivering gelatinous goo. Whichever came first.

Because even though ghosts are, of course, already dead, they can still feel pain, just as people who lose a limb can still feel it itching from time to time. Ghosts know, when you plunge a knife into their sternum, that it *should* hurt, and so it does. The wound will even bleed for a while.

Then, of course, they get over the shock of it, and the wound disappears. Which is discouraging, since the wounds they, in their turn, inflict upon me do not heal half so fast.

But whatever. It works. More or less.

The wound Maria de Silva had inflicted on me wasn't visible, but that didn't matter. What I was going to do to her certainly would be. With any luck, that husband of hers would be around and I could do the same to him.

And what was going to happen if things didn't work out that way, and the two of them got the best of me?

Well, that was the coolest part of the whole thing: I didn't even care. Really. I had cried out every last ounce of emotion in me, and now, I simply didn't care. It didn't matter. It really didn't.

I was numb.

So numb that, when I swung my legs out my bedroom window and landed on the roof of the front porch—my usual form of exit when I didn't want anyone inside to be aware I was up to something—I didn't even care about the things that normally really mean stuff to me, like the moon, for instance, hanging over the bay, casting everything into black-and-gray shadow, and the scent of the giant pine to one side of the porch. It didn't matter. None of it mattered.

I had just crossed the porch roof and was preparing to swing down from it when a glow that was brighter than the moon but much weaker than, say, the overhead in my bedroom, appeared behind me.

Okay, I'll admit it. I thought it was Jesse. Don't ask me why. I mean, it went against all logic. But whatever. My heart gave a happy lurch and I spun around. . . .

Maria was standing not five feet from me on the sloping, pine needle-strewn roof. She looked just as she had in that portrait over Clive Clemmings's desk: elegant and otherworldly.

Well, and why not? She isn't of this world, now, is she?

"Going somewhere, Susannah?" she asked me in her brittle, only slightly accented English.

"I was," I said, pushing my sweatshirt hood back. I had pulled my hair into a ponytail. Unattractive, I know, but I needed all the peripheral vision I could get. "But now that you're here, I see I don't have to. I can kick your bony butt here just as well as down at your stinking grave."

Maria raised her delicately arched black eyebrows. "Such language," she said. I swear, if she'd had a fan on her, she'd have been using it, just like Scarlett O'Hara. "And what could I possibly have done to warrant such an unladylike tongue-lashing? You'll catch more flies with honey, you know, than vinegar."

"You know good and well what you did," I said, taking a step toward her. "Let's start with the bugs in the orange juice."

She reached up and coyly smoothed back a strand of shining black hair that had escaped from her side ringlets.

"Yes," she said. "I thought you might like that one."

"But killing Dr. Clemmings?" I took another step forward. "That was even better. Because I imagine you didn't have to kill him at all, did you? You just wanted the painting, right? The one of Jesse?"

She made what in magazines they call a moue out of her mouth: You know, she kind of pursed her lips and looked pleased with herself at the same time.

"Yes," she said. "At first I wasn't going to kill him. But when I saw the portrait—*my* portrait—above his desk, well, how could I not? He is not even related to me. Why should he have such a fine painting—and in his miserable little office, as well? That painting used to grace my dining room. It hung in splendor over a table with seating for twenty."

"Yeah, well," I said. "My understanding is that none of your descendants wanted it. Your kids turned out to be nothing but a bunch of lowlifes and goons. Sounds like your parenting skills left a bit to be desired."

For the first time, Maria actually looked annoyed. She started to say something, but I interrupted her.

"What I don't get," I said, "is what you wanted the painting for. The one of Jesse. I mean, what good is it to you? Unless you only took it to get me in trouble."

"Wouldn't that be reason enough?" Maria inquired with a sneer.

"I suppose so," I said. "Except that it didn't work."

"*Yet*," Maria said, with a certain amount of emphasis. "There is still time."

I shook my head. I just shook my head as I

looked at her. "Gosh," I said, mostly to myself. "Gosh, I'm going to hurt you."

"Oh, yes." Maria tittered behind one lace-gloved hand. "I forgot. You must be very angry with me. He's gone, isn't he? Hector, I mean. That must be a great blow for you. I know how *fond* you were of him."

I could have jumped her right then. I probably should have. But it occurred to me that she might, you know, have some information on Jesse—how he was, or even where he was. Lame, I know, but look at it this way: On top of the whole, you know, love thing, he was one of the best friends I ever had.

"Yeah," I said. "Well, I guess slave-runners aren't really my cup of tea. That is who you married instead, right? A slave-runner. Your father must have been so proud."

That wiped the grin right off her face.

"You leave my father out of this," she snarled.

"Oh, why?" I asked. "Tell me something, is he sore at you? Your dad, I mean. You know, for having Jesse killed? Because I imagine he would be. I mean, basically, thanks to you, the de Silva family line ran out. And your kids with that Diego dude turned out to be, as we've already discussed, major losers. I bet whenever you run into your dad out there, you know, on the spiritual plane, he doesn't even say hi anymore, does he? That's gotta hurt."

I'm not sure how much of that, if any, Maria actually understood. Still, she seemed plenty mad.

"You!" she cried. "I warned you! I told you to make your family stop with their digging, but did you listen to me? It is your fault you've lost your precious Hector. If you had only listened, he would be here still. But no. You think, because you are this mediator—this special person who can communicate with spirits—that you are better than us . . . better than me! But you are nothing—nothing, do you hear? Who are the Simons? Who are they? No one! I, Maria Teresa de Silva, am a descendant of royalty—of kings and princes!"

I just laughed. I mean, seriously. Come on.

"Oh, yeah," I said. "And that sure was some princely behavior, killing your boyfriend like that."

Maria's scowl was like a dark storm cloud over her head. "Hector died," she hissed in a scary voice, "because he dared to break off our betrothal. He thought to disgrace me in front of everyone. Me! Knowing, as he did, of the royal lineage running through my blood. To suggest that I would—"

Whoa. This was a new one. "Wait a minute. He did *what*?"

But Maria was off on a rant.

"As if I, Maria de Silva, would allow myself to be so humiliated. He sought to return my letters and asked for his own—and his ring—back. He could not, he said, marry me, after what he had heard about me and Diego." She laughed, not pleasantly. "As if he did not know to whom he was speaking! As if he did not know he was speaking to a de Silva!"

I cleared my throat. "Um," I said. "I'm pretty sure he knew. I mean, that was his last name, too. Weren't the two of you cousins or something?"

Maria made a face. "Yes. I am ashamed to say I shared a name—and grandparents—with that—" She called Jesse something in Spanish that did not sound at all flattering. "He did not know with whom he was trifling. There was not a man in the county who would not have killed for the honor of marrying me."

"And it certainly appears," I couldn't help pointing out, "that at least one man in the county was killed for refusing that honor."

"Why shouldn't he have died?" Maria demanded.

"For insulting me in such a manner?"

"Um," I said, "how about because murder is illegal? And because having a guy killed because he doesn't want to marry you is the act of a freaking lunatic, which is exactly what you are. Funny how that part didn't trickle down through the annals of history. But don't worry. I'll make sure I get the word out."

Maria's face changed. Before, she'd looked disgusted and irritated. Now she looked murderous.

Which was kind of funny. If this chick thought anybody in the world cared about what some prissy broad had done a century and a half ago, she was mightily mistaken. She had managed to kill the one person to whom this piece of information might have been remotely interesting—Dr. Clive Clemmings, Ph.D.

But she was still apparently high on the whole we-de Silvas-are-descended-from-Spanish-royalty thing, since she whirled on me, petticoats flying, and went, in this scary voice, "Stupid girl! I said to Diego that you were far too much of a fool to cause trouble for us, but I see now that I was wrong. You are everything I have heard about mediators—interfering, loathsome creature!"

I was flattered. I truly was. No one had ever called me loathsome before.

"If *I'm* loathsome," I said, "what does that make you? Oh, wait, don't tell me, I already know. A two-faced backstabbing bitch, right?"

The next thing I knew, she'd pulled that knife from her sleeve and was once more pointing it at my throat.

"I will not stab you in the back," Maria assured me. "It is your face I intend to carve."

"Go ahead," I said. I reached out and seized the wrist of the hand that was clutching the knife. "You want to know what your big mistake was?" She grunted as, with a neat move I'd learned in tae kwan do, I twisted her arm behind her back. "Saying my losing Jesse was my fault. Because I was feeling sorry for you before. But now I'm just mad."

Then, sinking one knee into Maria de Silva's spine, I sent her sprawling, facedown, onto the porch roof.

"And when I'm mad," I said as I pried the knife from her fingers with my free hand, "I don't really know what comes over me. But I just sort of start hitting people. Really, really hard."

Maria wasn't taking any of this quietly. She was shrieking her head off—mostly in Spanish, though, so I just ignored her. I was the only one who could hear her, anyway.

"I told my mom's therapist about it," I informed her as I flung the knife, as hard as I could, into the backyard, still keeping her pinned down with the weight of my knee. "And you know what she said? She said the trigger to my rage mechanism is oversensitive."

Now that I was rid of the knife, I leaned forward and, with the hand I wasn't using to keep Maria's arm bent back against her spine, I seized a handful of those glossy black ringlets and jerked her head toward me.

"But you know what I said to her?" I asked Maria. "I said, it's not that the trigger to my rage mechanism is oversensitive. It's that people . . . just . . . keep . . . pissing . . . me . . . off."

To emphasize each of the last six syllables of that sentence, I rammed Maria de Silva's face into the roof tiles. When I dragged her head up after the sixth time, she was bleeding heavily from the nose and mouth. I observed this with great detachment, like it was someone else who had caused it and not me.

"Oh," I said. "Look at that. That is just so interfering and loathsome of me."

Then I smashed her face against the roof a few more times, saying, "This one is for jumping me while I was asleep and *holding a knife to my throat.* And this one is for making Dopey *eat bugs*, and this one is for making me have to clean up *bug guts*, and this one is for killing *Clive*, and oh yeah, this one is for *Jesse*—"

I won't say I was out of my mind with rage. I was mad. I was plenty mad. But I knew exactly what I was doing.

And it wasn't pretty. Hey, I'll be the first to admit that. I mean, violence is never the answer, right? Unless, of course, the person you're beating on is already dead.

But just because a hundred and fifty years ago this chick had had a good friend of mine offed, for no other reason than that he had very rightly wanted out of a marriage with her, she didn't deserve to have her face bashed in.

No way. What she deserved was to have every bone in her body broken.

Unfortunately, however, when I finally let go of Maria's hair and stood up to do just that, I noticed a sudden glow to my left.

Jesse, I thought, my heart doing another one of those speeding-up, skidding things.

But, of course, it wasn't Jesse. When I turned my head, what I saw materializing there was a very tall man in a dark mustache and goatee, dressed in clothes that were somewhat similar to Jesse's, only a lot fancier—like he was a costume party Zorro or something. His snug black trousers had this elaborate silver filigree pattern going down the side of each leg, and his white shirt had those puffy sleeves pirates always wear in movies. He had a lot of silver scrollwork on his holster, too, and all around the brim of his black cowboy hat.

And he didn't look very happy to see me.

"Okay," I said, putting my hands on my hips. "Wait, don't tell me. Diego, am I right?"

Under the pencil-thin mustache, his upper lip curled.

"I thought I told you," he said to Maria, who was sitting up and holding her sleeve to her bleeding nose, "to leave this one to me."

Maria was making a lot of very unattractive snuffling noises. You could tell she'd never had her nose broken before, because she wasn't tipping her head back to stop the bleeding.

Amateur.

"I thought she might be more amusing," Maria said in a voice laced with pain—and regret—"to play with."

Diego shook his head disgustedly. "No," he said. "With mediators we do not play. I thought that was made clear to you from the start. They are entirely too dangerous."

"I'm sorry, Diego." Maria's voice took on a whiny quality I had not heard before. I realized she was one of those girls who has a "guy" voice, one she uses only when men are around. "I should have done as you said."

It was my turn to be disgusted.

"Hello," I said to Maria. "This is the twenty-first century. Women are allowed to think for themselves now, you know."

Maria just glared at me over the sleeve she was holding to her bleeding nose.

"Kill her for me," she said in that whiny little-girl voice.

Diego took a step toward me, wearing an expression that told me he was only too happy to oblige his lady love.

"Oh, what?" I said. I wasn't even scared. I didn't care anymore. The numbness in my heart had pretty much taken over my whole body. "You always do what she tells you? You know, we have a word for that now. It's called being whipped."

Apparently, he was either unacquainted with this expression, or he just didn't care, since he kept coming at me. Diego was wearing spurs, and they clanged ominously against the roof tiles as he approached.

"You know," I said, holding my ground. "I gotta

tell you. The goatee thing? Yeah, way over. And you know a little jewelry really does go a long way. Just something you might want to consider. I'm actually glad you stopped by, because I have a couple things I've been meaning to say to you. Number one, about your wife? Yeah, she's a skank. And number two, you know that whole thing where you killed Jesse and then buried his remains out back there? Yeah, way uncool. Because you see, now I have to—"

Only I never got a chance to tell Felix Diego what I was going to have to do to him. That's because he interrupted me. He said in this deep and surprisingly menacing voice, for a guy with a goatee, "It has long been my conviction that the only good mediator is a dead one."

Then, before I could so much as twitch, he threw his arms around me. I thought he was trying to give me a hug or something, which would have been pretty weird.

But that wasn't what he was doing at all. No, what he was doing, actually, was throwing me off the porch roof.

Oh, yes. He threw me right into the hole where the hot tub was supposed to go. Right where they'd uncovered Jesse's remains, just that afternoon . . .

Which I thought was kind of ironic, actually. At least, while I was still capable of thought.

Which wasn't for long, since I lost consciousness shortly after slamming into the ground.

chapter *ten*

Here's the thing about mediators:

We're hard to kill.

I'm serious. You wouldn't believe the number of times I've been knocked down, dragged, stomped on, punched, kicked, bitten, clawed, whacked on the head, held underwater, shot at and, oh yeah, thrown off roofs.

But have I ever died? Have I ever sustained a life-threatening injury?

No. I've broken bones—plenty of them. I've got scars galore.

But the fact is, whoever—or whatever—created us mediators did give us one natural weapon, at least, to use in our fight against the undead. No, not superhuman strength, though that would have been handy. No, what we've got, Father Dom and I—and Jack, too, probably, although I doubt he's had an opportunity to test it out yet—is a hide tough enough to take all the abuse that gets heaped on us and then some.

Which was why even though by rights a fall like the one I took should have killed me, it didn't. Not even close.

Not, of course, that Maria de Silva and her paramour didn't think they'd been successful. They must have, or they'd have stuck around to finish the job. But when I woke up hours later, groggy and with a headache you would not believe, they were nowhere to be seen.

Clearly, I had won the first round. Well, in a manner of speaking, anyway. I mean, I wasn't dead, and that, in my book, is always a plus.

What I was, was concussed. I knew right away because I get them all the time. Concussions, I mean.

Well, all right, twice.

Anyway, it's not so pleasant, being concussed. Basically, you feel pukey and sore all over, but, not surprisingly, your head really hurts more than anything. In my case, it was even worse in that I'd been lying at the bottom of that hole for so long, the dew had had a chance to fall. It had collected on my clothes and soaked them through and made them feel very heavy. So dragging myself out of that pit Andy and Dopey had dug became a real chore.

In fact, it was dawn before I finally managed to let myself back into the house—thank God Sleepy had left the front door unlocked when he'd come in from his big date. Still, I had to climb all those stairs. It was pretty slow going. At least when I got to my room and was finally able to peel off all of my sodden, muddy clothes, I didn't have to worry, for once, about Jesse seeing me in my altogether.

Because, of course, Jesse was gone.

I tried not to think about that as I crawled into bed and shut my eyes. This strategy—the not-thinking-about-Jesse-being-gone strategy—seemed to work pretty well. I was asleep, I think, before that thought had really had a chance to sink in again.

I didn't wake up until well past eight. Apparently Sleepy had tried to get me up for work, but I was too far gone. They let me sleep in, I guess, because they all assumed I was still upset about what had happened the day before, about the skeleton they'd found in the backyard.

I only wish that was all I had to be upset about.

When the phone rang a little after nine, and Andy called up the stairs that it was for me, I was already up, standing in my bathroom in my sweats, examining the enormous bruise that had developed beneath my bangs. I looked like an alien. I'm not kidding. It was a wonder, really, I hadn't broken my neck. I was convinced that Maria and her boyfriend thought that's exactly what I'd done. It was the only reason I was still alive. The two of them were so cocky, they hadn't stuck around to make sure I was well and truly dead.

They'd obviously never met a mediator before. It takes a lot more than a fall off a roof to kill one of us.

"Susannah." Father Dominic's voice, when I picked up the phone, was filled with concern. "Thank God you're all right. I was so worried. . . . But you didn't, did you? Go to the cemetery last night?"

"No," I said. There hadn't been any reason to go there, in the end. The cemetery had come to me.

But I didn't say that to Father D. Instead, I asked, "Are you back in town?"

"I'm back. You didn't tell them, did you? Your family, I mean."

"Um," I said uncertainly.

"Susannah, you must. You really must. They have a right to know. We're dealing with a very serious haunting here. You could be killed, Susannah—"

I refrained from mentioning that I'd actually already come pretty close.

At that moment, the call-waiting went off. I said, "Father D., can you hold on a second?" and hit the receiver.

A high-pitched, vaguely familiar voice spoke in my ear, but for the life of me, I could not place it right away.

"Suze? Is that you? Are you all right? Are you sick or something?"

"Um," I said, extremely puzzled. "Yeah. I guess. Sort of. Who is this?"

The voice said, very indignantly, "It's me! Jack!"

Oh, God. Jack. Work. Right.

"Jack," I said. "How did you get my home number?"

"You gave it to Paul," Jack said. "Yesterday. Don't you remember?"

I did not, of course. All I could really remember from yesterday was that Clive Clemmings was dead, Jesse's portrait was missing . . .

And that Jesse, of course, was gone. Forever.

Oh, and the whole part where the ghost of

Felix Diego tried to split my head open.

"Oh," I said. "Yeah. Okay. Look, Jack, I have someone on the other—"

"Suze," Jack interrupted. "You were supposed to teach me to do underwater somersaults today."

"I know," I said. "I'm really sorry. I just . . . I just really couldn't face coming in to work today, bud. I'm sorry. It's nothing against you or anything. I just really need a day off."

"You sound so sad," Jack said, sounding pretty sad himself. "I thought you'd be really happy."

"You did?" I wondered if Father D. was still waiting on the other line or if he'd hung up in a huff. I was, I realized, treating him pretty badly. After all, he'd cut his little retreat short for me. "How come?"

"On account of how I—"

That's when I saw it. Just the faintest glow, over by the daybed. Jesse? Again my heart gave one of those lurches. It was really getting pathetic, how much I kept hoping, every time I saw the slightest shimmer, that it would be Jesse.

It wasn't.

It wasn't Maria or Diego either—thank God. Surely not even they would be bold enough to try to take a whack at me in broad daylight. . . .

"Jack," I said into the phone. "I have to go."

"Wait, Suze, I—"

But I'd hung up. That's because sitting there on my daybed, looking deeply unhappy, was Dr. Clive Clemmings, Ph.D.

Just my luck: Wish for a Jesse. Get a Clive.

"Oh," he said, blinking behind the lenses of his Coke-bottle-bottom glasses. He seemed almost as surprised to see me as I was to see him materialize there in my bedroom. "It's *you.*"

I just shook my head. Sometimes my bedroom feels like Grand Central Station.

"Well, I simply didn't—" Clive Clemmings fiddled with his bow tie. "I mean, when they said I should contact a mediator, I didn't . . . I mean, I never expected—"

"—that the mediator would be me," I finished for him. "Yeah. I get that a lot."

"It's only," Clive said apologetically, "that you're so . . ."

I just glared at him. I really wasn't in the mood. Can you blame me? What with the concussion, and all? "That I'm so what?" I demanded. "Female? Is that it? Or are you going to try to convince me you're shocked by my preternatural intelligence?"

"Er," Clive Clemmings said. "Young. I meant that . . . it's just that you're so young."

I sank down onto the window seat. Really, what had I ever done to deserve this? I mean, nobody wants to be visited by the specter of a guy like Clive. I'm almost positive nobody ever wanted him to visit when he was alive. So why me?

Oh, yeah. The mediator thing.

"To what do I owe the pleasure, Clive?" I probably should have called him Dr. Clemmings, but I had too much of a headache to be respectful of my elders.

"Well, I hardly know," Clive said. "I mean, suddenly, Mrs. Lampbert—that's my receptionist, don't you know?—she isn't answering when I call her, and when people telephone for me, well, she tells them . . . the most horrible thing, actually. I simply don't know what's come over her." Clive cleared his throat. "You see, she's saying that I'm—"

"Dead," I finished for him.

Clive eyes grew perceptibly bigger behind his glasses.

"Why," he said, "that's extraordinary. How could you know that? Well, yes, of course, you are the mediator, after all. They said you'd understand. But really, Miss Ackerman, I've had the most trying few days. I don't feel at all like myself, and I—"

"That," I interrupted him, "is because you're dead."

Ordinarily, I might have been a little nicer about it, but I guess I still felt a little kernel of resentment toward old Clive for his cavalier dismissal of my suggestion that Jesse might have been murdered.

"But that's not possible," Clive said. He tugged on his bow tie. "I mean, look at me. I am clearly here. You are speaking to me—"

"Yeah," I said. "Because I'm a mediator, Clive. That's my job. To help people like you move on after they've . . . you know." Since he clearly did not know, I elaborated: "Croaked."

Clive blinked rapidly several times in succession. "I . . . I . . . Oh, dear."

"Yeah," I said. "See? Now let's see if we can figure out why you're here and not in happy historian heaven. What's the last thing you remember?"

Clive dropped his hand from his chin. "Pardon?"

"What's the last thing you remember," I repeated, "from before you found yourself . . . well, invisible to Mrs. Lampbert?"

"Oh." Clive reached up to scratch his bald head. "Well, I was sitting at my desk, and I was looking at those letters you brought me. Quite kind of your stepfather to think of us. People so often overlook their community's historical society, when you know, really, without us, the fabric of the local lore would be permanently—"

"Clive," I said. I knew I sounded cranky, but I couldn't help it. "Look, I haven't even had breakfast yet. Can you get a move on, please?"

"Oh." He blinked some more. "Yes. Of course. Well, as I was saying, I was examining the letters you brought me. Ever since you left my office the other day, I've been thinking about what you said . . . about Hector de Silva, I mean. It does seem a bit unlikely that a fellow who wrote so lovingly of his family would simply walk out on them without a word. And the fact that you found Maria's letters buried in the yard of what was once a well-known boardinghouse . . . Well, I must say, upon further consideration, the whole thing struck me as extremely odd. I'd picked up my dictaphone and was just making a few notes for Mrs. Lampbert to type up later when I suddenly felt . . . well, a chill. As if someone had turned the air-conditioning up very high. Although I can assure you Mrs. Lampbert knows better than that. Some of our artifacts must be kept in highly controlled atmospheric climates, and she would never—"

"It wasn't the air-conditioning," I said flatly.

He stared at me, clearly startled. "No. No, it wasn't. Because a moment later, I caught the faintest whiff of orange blossoms. And you know Maria Diego was quite well-known for wearing orange blossom–scented toilet water. It was so odd. Because a second later, I could swear that for a moment . . . " The look in his eyes, behind the thick lenses of those glasses, grew faraway. "Well, for a moment, I could have sworn I saw her. Just out of the corner of my eye. Maria de Silva Diego . . . "

The faraway look left his eyes. When his gaze next fastened onto mine, it was laser sharp.

"And then I felt," he told me, in a tightly controlled voice, "a shooting pain, all up and down my arm. I knew what it was, of course. Congenital heart disease runs in my family. It killed my grandfather, you know, shortly after his book was first published. But I, unlike him, have been extremely diligent with my diet and exercise regimen. It could only have been the shock, you know, of seeing—thinking I was seeing, anyway—something that wasn't—that couldn't possibly—"

He broke off, then continued, "Well, I reached for the telephone to call 911 at once, but it . . . well, the telephone sort of . . . leaped off my desk."

I just looked at him. I had to admit, by this

time I was feeling sorry for him. I mean, he had been murdered, just like Jesse. And by the same hand, too. Well, more or less.

"I couldn't reach it," Clive said sadly. "The telephone, I mean. And that . . . that's the last thing I remember."

I licked my lips. "Clive," I said. "What were you saying? Into the dictaphone. Right before you saw her. Maria de Silva, I mean."

"What was I saying? Oh, of course. I was saying that though it would bear further investigation, it did seem to me as if what you suggested, and what my grandfather always believed, might possibly have merit. . . ."

I shook my head. I couldn't believe it.

"She killed you," I murmured.

"Oh." Clive was no longer blinking or tugging on his bow tie. He just sat there, looking like a scarecrow somebody had pulled the pole out from under. "Yes. I suppose you could say that. But only in a manner of speaking. I mean, it was the shock, after all. But it's not as if she—"

"To keep you from telling anyone what I said." In spite of my headache, I was getting mad all over again. "And she probably killed your grandfather, too, the same way."

Clive did blink then, questioningly. "My . . . my

grandfather? You think so? Well, I must say . . . I mean, his death was rather sudden, but there was no sign of—" His expression changed. "Oh. Oh, I see. You think my grandfather was killed by the ghost of Maria de Silva Diego to keep him from writing further about his theory concerning her cousin's disappearance?"

"That's one way of putting it," I said. "She didn't want him going around telling the truth about what happened to Jesse."

"Jesse?" Clive echoed. "Who is Jesse?"

We were both nearly startled out of our wits by a sudden knock on my door.

"Suze?" my stepfather called. "Can I come in?"

Clive, in a flurry of agitation, dematerialized. I said come in, and the door opened, and Andy stood there, looking awkward. He never comes into my room, except occasionally to fix things.

"Uh, Suze?" he said. "Yeah, um, you have a visitor. Father Dominic is—"

Andy didn't finish because Father Dominic appeared just behind him.

I can't really explain why I did what I did then. There is no other explanation for it other than the simple fact that, well, in the six months I'd known him, I'd come to really feel something for the old guy.

In any case, at the sight of him, I jumped up from the window seat, completely involuntarily, and hurled myself at him. Father Dominic looked more than a little surprised at this unbridled display of emotion, as I am normally somewhat reserved.

"Oh, Father D.," I said into Father Dominic's shirt-front. "I'm so glad to see you."

I was, too. Finally—*finally*—some normalcy was returning to my world, which seemed to have gone into a complete tailspin in the past twenty-four hours. Father Dominic was back. Father Dominic would take care of everything. He always did. Just standing there with my arms around him and my head against his chest, smelling his priestly smell, which was of Woolite and, more faintly, the cigarette he'd snuck in the car on his way over, I felt like everything was going to be all right.

"Oh," Father Dominic said. I could feel his voice reverberating inside his chest, along with the small noises his stomach was making as it digested whatever it was he'd scarfed down for breakfast. "Dear." Father Dom patted me awkwardly on the shoulder.

Behind us, I heard Dopey say, "What's with *her*?"

Andy told him to be quiet.

"Aw, come on," Dopey said. "She can't still be upset over that stupid skeleton we found. I mean, that kind of thing shouldn't bother the Queen of the Night Peo—"

Dopey broke off with a cry of pain. I glanced around Father D.'s shoulder and saw Andy pulling his second-oldest son down the hallway by the rim of his ear.

"Cut it out, Dad," Dopey was bellowing. "Ow! Dad, cut it out!"

A door slammed. Down the hall in Dopey's room, Andy was reading him the riot act.

I let go of Father D.

"You've been smoking," I said.

"Just a little," he admitted. Seeing my expression, he shrugged helplessly. "Well, it was a long drive. And I was certain that by the time I got here, I'd find you all murdered in your beds. You really have the most alarming way, Susannah, of getting yourself into scrapes. . . ."

"I know." I sighed, and went to sit on the window seat, circling one knee with my arms. I was in sweats, and I hadn't bothered putting on make-up or even washing my hair. What was the point?

Father D. didn't seem to notice my heinous appearance. He went on, as if we were back in his office, discussing student government fund-raising, or something completely innocuous like that, "I've brought some holy water. It's in my car. I'll tell your stepfather that you asked me to bless the house, on account of yesterday's, er, discovery. He might wonder at your suddenly embracing the Church, but you'll just have to start insisting upon saying grace at supper time—or perhaps even attending Mass from time to time—to convince him of your sincerity. I've been doing a bit of reading on those two—Maria de Silva and this Diego person—and they were quite devout. Murderers, it appears, but also churchgoers. They will, I think, be quite reluctant to enter a home that has been sanctified by a priest." Father Dominic looked down at me with concern. "It's what could happen when you set foot anywhere outside this house that's worrying me. The minute you—Good heavens, Susannah." Father Dominic broke off and peered down at me curiously. "What on earth happened to your forehead?"

I reached up and touched the bruise beneath my bangs.

"Oh," I said, wincing a little. The wound was still tender. "Nothing. Look, Father D.—"

"That isn't nothing." Father Dominic took a step forward, then inhaled sharply. "Susannah!

Where in heaven's name did you get that nasty bruise?"

"It's nothing," I said, scraping my bangs down over my eyes. "It's just a little token of Felix Diego's esteem."

"That mark is hardly nothing," Father Dominic declared. "Susannah, has it occurred to you that you might have a concussion? We should have that X-rayed immediately—"

"Father Dominic—"

"No arguments, Susannah," Father D. said. "Put some shoes on. I'm going to go have a word with your stepfather, and then we're going down to the Carmel Hosp—"

The phone jangled noisily. I told you. Grand Central Station. I picked it up, mostly to give myself time to think of an excuse why I didn't need to go to the hospital. A trip to the emergency room was going to require a story about how I'd come to obtain this latest injury, and frankly, I was running out of good lies.

"Hello?" I said into the receiver while Father D. scowled down at me.

"Suze?" That all-too-familiar high-pitched little voice. "It's me again. Jack."

"Jack," I said tiredly. "Look, I told you before. I'm really not feeling well—"

"That's just it," Jack said. "I got to thinking that maybe you hadn't heard. And then I thought I'd call and tell you. Because I know you'll feel better when I tell you."

"Tell me what, Jack?"

"About how I mediated that ghost for you," Jack said.

God, my head was pounding. I was so not in the mood for this. "Oh, yeah? What ghost was that, Jack?"

"You know," Jack said. "That guy who was bugging you. That Hector guy."

I nearly dropped the phone. I did drop it, actually, but I flung out my hands and caught the receiver before it hit the floor. Then I held it back up to my ear with both hands so I would be sure not to drop it again—and make certain I was hearing him right. I did all this with Father Dominic watching me.

"Jack," I said, feeling like all the wind had been knocked out of me. "What are you talking about?"

"That guy," Jack said. His childish lisp had gone indignant. "You know, the one who wouldn't leave you alone. That lady Maria told me—"

"Maria?" I had forgotten all about my headache, all about Father Dom. I practically yelled into the phone, "Jack, what are you talking about? Maria who?"

"That old-fashioned lady ghost," Jack said, sounding taken aback. And why not? I was shouting like a lunatic. "The nice one whose picture was in that bald guy's office. She told me that this Hector guy—the one from the other picture, the little picture—was bugging you, and that if I wanted to give you a nice surprise, I should exer—I should exor—I should—"

"Exorcise him?" My knuckles had gone white around the receiver. "Exorcise him, Jack? Is that what you did?"

"Yeah," Jack said, sounding pleased with himself. "Yeah, that's what it was. I exorcised him."

chapter eleven

I sank down onto the window seat.

"What—" My lips felt numb. I don't know if it was a complication of my concussion or what, but all of a sudden I couldn't feel my lips. "What did you say, Jack?"

"I exorcised him for you." Jack sounded immensely pleased with himself. "All by myself, too. Well, that lady helped a little. Did it work? Is he gone?"

Across my room, Father Dominic was looking at me questioningly. Small wonder. My conversation, from his end, had to sound completely bizarre. I hadn't, after all, had a chance to tell him about Jack.

"Suze?" Jack said. "Are you still there?"

"When?" I murmured through my numb lips.

Jack went, "What?"

"When, Jack," I said. "When did you do this?"

"Oh. Last night. While you were out with my brother. See, that Maria lady, she came over, and she brought that picture, and some candles, and then she told me what to say, and so I said it, and it was really cool, because this red smoke started coming out of the candles, and then it swirled and swirled, and then over our heads this big hole opened up in the air, and I looked up inside it, and it was really dark, and then I said some more words, and then that guy appeared, and he got sucked up right inside."

I didn't say anything. What could I say? The kid had just described an exorcism—at least, all the ones I'd ever experienced. He wasn't making it up. He had exorcised Jesse. He had exorcised *Jesse*. Jesse had been *exorcised*.

"Suze," Jack said. "Suze, are you still there?"

"I'm still here," I said. I guess I must have looked pretty awful, since Father Dom came and sat down on the window seat next to me, looking all worried.

And why not? I was in shock.

And this was a different kind of shock than I'd

ever felt before. This wasn't like being thrown off a roof or having a knife held to my throat. This was worse.

Because I couldn't believe it. I simply couldn't believe it. Jesse had kept his promise. He hadn't disappeared because his remains had, at long last, been found, proving he'd been murdered. He'd disappeared because Maria de Silva had had him exorcised. . . .

"You're not mad at me, are you?" Jack asked worriedly. "I mean, I did the right thing, right? That Maria lady said Hector was really mean to you, and you would be really thankful—" There was a noise in the background, and then Jack said, "That's Caitlin. She wants to know when you're coming back. She wants to know if you can maybe come in this afternoon, because she has to—"

But I never did learn what Caitlin had to do. That's because I had hung up. I just couldn't listen to that sweet little voice telling me these horrible, awful things for one second more.

The thing was, it wouldn't sink in. It just wouldn't. I understood intellectually what Jack had just said, but emotionally, it wasn't registering.

Jesse had *not* moved on from this plane to the next—not of his own free will. He had been ripped from his existence here the same way he'd been ripped from life and, ultimately, by the very same hands.

And why?

For the same reason he'd been killed: to keep him from embarrassing Maria de Silva.

"Susannah." Father Dominic's voice was gentle. "Who is Jack?"

I glanced up, startled. I had practically forgotten Father D. was in the room. But he wasn't just in the room. He was sitting right beside me, his blue eyes filled with bewildered concern.

"Susannah," he said. Father Dom never calls me Suze, like everyone else does. I asked him why once, and he told me it was because he thought Suze sounded vulgar. Vulgar! That really cracked me up at the time. He's so funny, so old-fashioned.

Jesse never called me Suze, either.

"Jack's a mediator," I said. "He's eight years old. I've been babysitting for him up at the resort."

Father Dominic looked surprised. "A mediator? Really? How extraordinary." Then his look of surprise turned back to one of concern. "You ought to have called me straightaway, Susannah, the moment you realized it. There aren't many mediators in the world. I would like very much to speak to him. Show him the ropes, as it were. You know, there's such a lot to learn for a young mediator. It mightn't be wise for you to undertake educating one, Susannah, given your own comparative youth. . . ."

"Yeah," I said with a bitter laugh. To my bemusement, the sound caught in my throat on a sort of sob. "You can say that again."

I couldn't believe it. I was crying again.

What *was* this, anyway? I mean, this crying thing? I go for months dry as a bone, and then all of a sudden, I'm weeping at the drop of a hat.

"Susannah." Father Dominic reached out and grabbed my arm. He gave me a little shake. I could tell by his expression he was really astonished. Like I said, I never cry. "Susannah, what is it? Are you *crying*, Susannah?"

I could only nod.

"But why, Susannah?" Father Dom asked urgently. "Why? Jesse? It's a hard thing, and I know you'll miss him, but—"

"You don't understand," I blurted. I was having trouble seeing. Everything had gotten very fuzzy. I couldn't see my bed or even the patterns on the pillows on the window seat, and they were much closer. I raised my hands to my face, thinking maybe Father Dom had been right, and that I should get that X ray after all. Something was evidently wrong with my vision.

But when my fingers encountered wetness on my cheeks, I was forced to admit the truth. There wasn't anything wrong with my vision. My eyes were simply overflowing with tears.

"Oh, Father," I said, and for the second time in half an hour, I threw my arms around a priest's neck. My forehead collided with his glasses, and they went all crooked. To say that Father Dominic was startled by this gesture would be an understatement of the grossest kind.

But judging by the way he froze up when I uttered them, he was even more surprised by the words that came out of my mouth.

"He exorcised Jesse, Father D. Maria de Silva tricked him into doing it. She told Jack that Jesse had been b-bothering me, and that he'd b-be doing me a favor, getting rid of him. Oh, Father Dominic—" My voice rose to a wail. "What am I going to do?"

Poor Father Dominic. I highly doubt he has hysterically weeping women throwing their arms around him all that often. You can totally tell. He didn't know how to react at all. I mean, he patted me on the shoulder and said, "Shhh, everything will be all right," and stuff, but you could tell he was really uncomfortable. I guess he was afraid Andy was going to walk by and think I was crying because of something Father Dominic had said.

Which was ridiculous, of course. As if anything anybody *said* could make me cry.

After a few minutes of Father Dom saying, "Shhh, everything will be all right," and being all stiff, I couldn't help laughing.

Seriously. I mean, it was funny. In a sad, pathetic kind of way.

"Father Dominic," I said, pulling away and looking up at him through my streaming eyes. "Are you joking? Everything is *not* going to be all right. Okay? Nothing is *ever* going to be all right *ever* again."

Father Dominic might not have been a very good hugger, but he was all there in the hanky department. He fished his out and started dabbing my face with it. I'd seen him do this before with the little kids at school, the kindergartners who were crying over dropped ice-cream cones or whatever. He really had the whole dabbing thing down.

"Now, Susannah," he said as he dabbed. "That isn't true. You know that isn't true."

"Father," I said. "I know it is true. Jesse is gone, and it is totally my fault."

"How is it your fault?" Father Dominic looked down at me disapprovingly. "Susannah, it isn't your fault at all."

"Yes, it is. You said so yourself. I should have called you the minute I realized the truth about Jack. But I didn't. I thought I could handle him myself. I thought it was no big deal. And now look what happened. Jesse's gone. *Forever.*"

"It is a tragedy," Father Dominic said. "I cannot think of a greater injustice. Jesse was a very good friend to you . . . to both of us. But the fact is, Susannah"—He'd managed to clean up almost all my tears, and now he put his handkerchief away—"he spent a good many years wandering in a sort of half-life. Now his struggles are over, and he can perhaps begin to enjoy his just rewards."

I narrowed my eyes at him. What was he *talking* about?

He must have read the skepticism in my face, since he said, "Well, think about it, Susannah. For one hundred and fifty years, Jesse was trapped in a sort of netherworld between his past life and his next. Though you can lament the manner in which it happened, he has, at last, made the leap to his final destination—"

I jerked away from Father D. In fact, I jerked

away from the window seat. I stood up, strode away a few paces, and then whirled around, astounded by what I'd just heard.

"What are you talking about?" I demanded. "Jesse was here for a *reason*. I don't know what it was, and I'm not sure he did either. But whatever it was, he was supposed to stay here, in this 'netherworld,' until he'd worked it out. Now he'll never be able to. Now he'll never know why he was here for all that time."

"I understand that, Susannah," Father Dominic said in a voice I found infuriatingly calm. "And as I said before, it is unfortunate—a tragedy. But regardless, Jesse has moved on, and we should at least be glad he's found eternal peace—"

"Oh my *God*!" I was shouting again, but I didn't care. I was enraged. "Eternal peace? How do you *know* that's what he's found? You can't know that."

"No," Father Dominic said. I could tell he was choosing his words with care now. Like I was a bomb that might go off if he used the wrong one.

"You're right," Father D. said quietly. "I can't know that. But that is the difference between you and me, Susannah. You see, I have faith."

I was across the room in three quick strides. I didn't know what I was going to do. I certainly wasn't going to hit him. I mean, the trigger to my anger mechanism might be oversensitive, but I'm not about to go around punching priests. Well, at least not Father Dom. He is my homeboy, as we used to say back in Brooklyn.

Still, I think I was going to shake him. I was going to put my hands on his shoulders and attempt to shake some sense in him, since reasoning did not appear to be working. I mean, seriously, faith. *Faith!* As if *faith* ever worked better than a good ass-kicking.

But before I could lay a hand on him, I heard someone behind me clear his throat. I looked around, and there was Andy, in his tool belt and jeans and a T-shirt that said WELCOME TO DUCK BILL FLATS, standing in my open doorway and looking concerned.

"Suze," he said. "Father Dominic. Is everything all right in here? I thought I heard some shouting."

Father Dominic stood up.

"Yes," he said, looking grave. "Well, Susannah is—and very rightly, too—concerned about the, er, unfortunate discovery in your backyard yesterday. She has asked me, Andrew, to perform a house blessing and I, of course, said I would. I've left my Bible in the car, however. . . . "

Andy perked right up. "You want me to go get

200

it for you, Father?" he asked.

"Oh, that would be wonderful, Andrew," Father D. said. "Just wonderful. It should be on the front seat. If you could bring that to me, I'll get to work straightaway."

"No problem, Father," Andy said, and he went away, looking all happy. Which is easy to be if you, like Andy, haven't the slightest clue what's going on in your own house. I mean, Andy doesn't believe. He doesn't know there's a plane of existence other than this one. He doesn't know people from that other plane are trying to kill me.

Or that I was once in love with the guy whose bones he dug up yesterday.

"Father D.," I said, the minute I heard Andy's feet hit the stairs.

"Susannah," he said tiredly. He was trying to head me off at the pass, I could tell. "I understand how difficult this is for you. Jesse was very special. I know he meant a great deal to you—"

I couldn't believe this. "Father D.—"

"—but the fact is, Susannah, Jesse is in a better place now." Father Dominic, as he spoke, walked across my room, stooped down by the door, and pulled out a black bag he'd apparently set down in the hallway. He lifted the bag, set it down again on my unmade bed, and opened it. Then he started taking things out of it.

"You and I," he went on, "are just going to have faith in that thought, and move on."

I put my hands on my hips. I don't know if it was the concussion or the fact that my boyfriend had been exorcised, but my bitch quotient was set on high, I think.

"I have faith, Father Dom," I informed him. "I have plenty of faith. I have faith in myself, and I have faith in you. That's how I know that we can fix this."

Father Dominic's baby blues widened behind the lenses of his bifocals as he lifted a purple ribbony thing to his lips, kissed it, then slipped it around his neck. "Fix this? Fix what? Whatever do you mean, Susannah?"

"You know what I mean," I said, because he did.

"I—" Father Dominic took a metal thing that looked like an ice-cream scooper out of his bag, along with a jar of what I could only suppose was holy water. "I realize, of course," he said, "that Maria de Silva Diego will have to be dealt with. That is troubling, but I think you and I are both perfectly well equipped to handle the situation. And the boy, Jack, will have to be seen to and adequately indoctrinated in the appropriate methods of mediation, of which exorcism, as you know, should only be used as a last resort. But—"

"That's not it," I said.

Father Dominic looked up from his house blessing preparation. "It isn't?" he echoed questioningly.

"No," I repeated. "And don't pretend like you don't know what I'm talking about."

He blinked a few times, reminding me of Clive Clemmings.

"I can't say that I do know, Susannah," he said. "What are you talking about?"

"Getting him back," I said.

"Getting who back, Susannah?" Father Dom's all-night driving marathon was starting to show. He looked tired. He was a handsome guy, for someone in his sixties. I was pretty sure half the nuns and most of the female portion of the Mission's congregation were in love with him. Not that Father D. would ever notice. The knowledge that he was a middle-aged hottie would only embarrass Father D.

"You know who," I said.

"Jesse? Getting Jesse back?" Father Dominic stood there, the stole around his neck and the dipper thing in one hand. He looked bewildered. "Susannah, you know as well as I do that once spirits find their way out of this world, we lose all contact with them. They're gone. They've moved on."

"I know. I didn't say it was going to be easy. In fact, I can think of only one way to do it, and even then, well, it'll be risky. But with your help, Father D., it just might work."

"My help?" Father Dominic looked confused. "My help with what?"

"Father D.," I said. "I want you to exorcise me."

chapter _twelve_

"For the last time, Susannah," Father Dominic said. This time he pounded on the steering wheel for emphasis as he said it. "What you are asking is impossible."

I rolled my eyes. "Hello? What happened to faith? I thought if you had faith, anything was possible."

Father D. didn't like having his own words tossed back at him. I could tell by the way he was grimacing at the reflection of the cars behind us in his rearview mirror.

"Then let me say that what you are suggesting has a very unlikely chance of succeeding." Driving in Carmel-by-the-Sea is no joke, since the houses have no numbers, and the tourists can't, for the life of them, figure out where they're going. And the traffic is, of course, ninety-eight percent tourists. Father D. was frustrated enough by our efforts to get where we were going. My announcement back in my bedroom that I wanted him to exorcise me wasn't helping his mood much, either.

"Not to mention the fact that it is unethical, immoral, and probably quite dangerous," he concluded, as he waved at a minivan to go ahead and go around us.

"Right," I said. "But it's not *impossible*."

"You seem to be forgetting something," Father D. said. "You are not a ghost, nor are you possessed by one."

"I know. But I *have* a spirit, right? I mean, a soul. So why can't you exorcise it? Then I can go, you know, have a look around, see if I can find him, and if I do, bring him back." I added as an afterthought, "If he wants to come, of course."

"Susannah." Father Dom was really fed up with me, you could totally tell. It had been all right, back at the house, when I'd been crying and everything. But then I'd gotten this terrific idea.

Only Father Dominic didn't think the idea was so terrific, see. I personally found it brilliant. I couldn't believe I hadn't thought of it before. I guess my brain had gotten a little squashed, what with the concussion.

But there was no reason why my plan shouldn't work. No reason at all.

Except that Father Dominic would have no part of it.

"No," he said. Which was what he'd been saying ever since I first mentioned it. "What you are suggesting, Susannah, has never been done before. There isn't the slightest guarantee it will work. Or that, if it does, you will be able to return to your body."

"That," I said calmly, "is where the rope comes in."

"No!" Father Dominic shouted.

He had to slam on the brakes at that very moment because a tour bus came barreling along from out of nowhere, and, there being no traffic lights in downtown Carmel, there were often differences of opinion over whose turn it was at four-way stops. I heard the holy water, still in its jar in his black bag on the backseat, slosh around.

You wouldn't have thought there'd be any left, what with the dousing Father D. had given our house. That stuff had been seriously flying. I hoped he was right about Maria and Felix being too Catholic to dare to cross the threshold of a newly blessed home. Because if he was wrong, I'd pretty much made a big ass out of myself in front of Dopey for no reason. Dopey had been all, "Whatcha doing *that* for, Father D.?" when Father Dominic got to his room with the aspergillum, which turned out to be what the dippy thing was called.

"Because your sister asked me to," Father Dom replied as he flicked holy water all over Dopey's weight bench—probably the only time that thing had ever come close to being cleaned.

"Suze asked you to bless my room?" I could hear Dopey's voice all the way down the hall, in my own room. I'm sure neither of them knew I was listening.

"She asked me to bless the house," Father Dominic said. "She was very disturbed by the discovery of the skeleton in your backyard, as I'm sure you know. I would greatly appreciate it if you would show her a little extra kindness for the next few days, Bradley."

Bradley! In my room, I started cracking up. Bradley! Who knew?

I don't know what Dopey said in reply to Father Dom's suggestion that he be nicer to me, because I took the opportunity to shower and change into civilized clothing. I figured twelve hours was more than enough to go around in sweats. Any more than that and you are, quite frankly, wallowing in your own sorrow. Jesse would not want my grieving over him to affect my by-now-famous sense of fashion.

Besides, I had a plan.

So it was that, showered, made up, and attired in what I considered to be the height of mediator chic in the form of a slip dress and sandals, I felt prepared to take on not only the minions of Satan but the staff at the *Carmel Pine Cone*, in front of whose office Father D. had promised to drop me. I had not only figured out, you see, a way to get Jesse back: I'd figured out a way to avenge Clive Clemmings's death, not to mention his grandfather's.

Oh, yes. I still had it. But good.

"It is out of the question, Susannah," Father Dominic said. "So put the idea from your head. Wherever he is now, Jesse is in a better place than he was. Let him rest there."

"Fine," I said. We pulled up in front of a low building, heavily shaded by pine trees. The offices of the local rag.

"Fine," Father Dominic said, putting his car into park. "I'll wait out here for you. It would probably be better if I didn't come in, I suppose."

"Probably," I said. "And there's no need to wait. I'll find my own way home." I undid my seat belt.

"Susannah," Father Dominic said.

I lifted my sunglasses and peered at him. "Yes?"

"I'll wait here for you," he said. "We still have a good deal of work to do, you and I."

I screwed up my face. "We do?"

"Maria and Diego," Father D. reminded me gently. "You are protected from them at home now, but they are still at large and will, I think, be excessively angry when they realize you are not dead."—I had finally broken down and explained to him what had happened to my head—"We need to make preparations, you and I, to deal with them."

"Oh," I said. "That."

I had, of course, forgotten all about it. Not because I did not feel Maria and her husband needed to be dealt with, but because I knew my idea of dealing with them and Father D.'s idea were not exactly going to gel. I mean, priests aren't really big on beating adversaries into bloody pulps. They're more into gentle reasoning.

"Sure," I said. "Yeah. We should get right on that."

"And, of course—" Father D. looked really odd.

I realized why when the next words that came out of his mouth were, "We've got to decide what's to be done with Jesse's remains."

Jesse's remains. The words hit me like twin punches. Jesse's remains. Oh, God.

"I was thinking," Father Dominic said, still choosing his words with elaborate care, "of putting in a formal request with the coroner's office to have the remains transferred to the church for burial in the Mission cemetery. Do you agree with me that that would be appropriate?"

Something hard grew in my throat. I tried to swallow it down.

"Yes," I said. It came out sounding funny, though. "What about a headstone?"

Father Dominic said, "Well, that might be difficult, seeing as how I highly doubt the coroner will be able to make a positive identification."

Right. They didn't have dental X rays back when Jesse'd been alive.

"Maybe," Father Dominic said, "a simple cross . . ."

"No," I said. "A headstone. I have three thousand dollars." More if I took back all those Jimmy Choos. Good thing I'd saved the receipts. Who needed a fall wardrobe, anyway? "Do you think that would cover it?"

"Oh," Father Dominic said, looking taken aback. "Susannah, I—"

"You can let me know," I said. Suddenly, I didn't think I could sit there on the street anymore, discussing this with him. I opened the passenger door. "I better go. See you in a few."

And I started to get out of the car.

But not soon enough. Father D. called my name again.

"Father D.," I began impatiently, but he held up a hand.

"Just hear me out, Susannah," he said. "It isn't that I don't wish there was something we could do to bring Jesse back. I, too, wish that he could, as you said, have found his own way to wherever it was he was supposed to have gone after death. I do. I truly do. I just don't think that going to the extreme you're suggesting is . . . well, necessary. And I certainly don't think it's what he would have wanted, your risking your life for his sake."

I thought about that. I really did. Father D. was absolutely right, of course. Jesse would not have wanted me to risk my life for him, not ever. Especially considering the fact that he doesn't even have one anymore. A life, I mean.

But let's face it, Jesse's from a slightly different era. Back when he was born, girls spent all their time at quilting bees. They didn't exactly go around routinely kicking butt the way we do now.

And even though Jesse's seen me kick butt a million times, it still makes him nervous, you can totally tell. You would think he'd be used to it by now, but no. I mean, he was even surprised when he heard about Maria and her knife. I guess that's kind of understandable. Come on, little Miss Hoopskirt, poppin' a blade?

Still, even after a century and a half of knowing she was the one who had ordered the hit on him, that completely blew his mind. I mean, that sexism thing, they drive that stuff down deep. It hasn't been easy, curing him of it.

Anyway, all I'm saying is, Father D.'s right: Jesse definitely would not want me to risk my life for him.

But we don't always get what we want, do we?

"Fine," I said again. You would have thought that Father D. would notice how accommodating I'd become all of a sudden. I mean, didn't he realize that he wasn't the only person in town who could help me? I had an ace up my sleeve, and he didn't even know it.

"Be back in a flash," I said with a full-on, hundred-watt smile.

Then I turned and went into the offices of the

Carmel Pine Cone like I was just going in there to place a personal ad or something.

What I was doing, of course, was something way more insidious.

"Is CeeCee Webb here?" I asked the pimply kid at the reception desk.

He looked up, startled. I don't know what freaked him out more, my slip dress or the fact that I'd asked to see CeeCee.

"Over there," he said, pointing. His voice wobbled all over the place.

"Thanks," I said, and started down a long and quite messy corridor, passing a lot of industrious journalists who were eagerly tapping out their stories on the recent spate of wind chime thefts off people's front porches, and the more alarming problem of parking in front of the post office.

CeeCee was in a cubicle in the back. It appeared to be the photocopier cubicle, because that was what she was doing: photocopying.

"Oh my God," she said, when she saw me. "What are you doing here?"

She didn't say it in an unhappy way, though.

"Slumming," I said, and settled myself into an office chair beside the fax machine.

"I can see that," CeeCee said. She was taking her role as girl reporter very seriously. Her long, stick-straight white hair was coiled up on top of her head with a number-two pencil, and there was a smudge of toner on one pink cheek. "Why aren't you at the resort?"

"Mental health day," I said. "On account of the dead body they found in our backyard yesterday."

CeeCee dropped a ream of paper.

"Oh my God!" she gushed. "That was *you*? I mean, there's a mention of a coroner's call up to the hills in the Police Beat section, but somebody said it must have been a Native American burial site or something. . . ."

"Oh, no," I said. "Not unless the Native Americans around here wore spurs."

"Spurs?" CeeCee reached for a notepad that was resting on top of the copier, then pulled the pencil from the knot on top of her head, causing her long hair to fall down around her shoulders. Because she is an albino, CeeCee keeps the vast majority of her skin protected from the sun at all times, even when she's working inside an office. Today was no exception. In spite of the heat outside, she was wearing jeans and a brown button-down sweater.

On the other hand, the air-conditioning in the place had to be on high. It was like an icebox in there.

"Spill," CeeCee said, perching on the edge of the table that supported the fax machine.

I did. I spilled it all. Everything, from the letters Dopey had found to my trip to Clive's office to his untimely death the day before. I mentioned Clive's grandfather's book and Jesse and the historically significant role my house had played in his murder. I told her about Maria and Diego and their no-account kids, the fact that Jesse's portrait was now missing from the historical society, and my suspicions that the skeleton found in my backyard belonged to him.

When I was through, CeeCee raised her gaze from the notepad and went, "Jeez, Simon. This could be a movie of the week."

"Lifetime channel," I agreed.

CeeCee pointed at me with the pencil. "Tiffani-Amber Thiessen could play Maria!"

"So," I said. "Are you going to print it?"

"Heck, yeah," CeeCee said. "I mean, it's got everything. Romance and murder and intrigue and local interest. Too bad almost everybody involved has been dead a hundred years or more. Still, if I can get confirmation from the coroner that your skeleton belonged to a male in his twenties . . . Any idea how they did it? Killed him, I mean?"

I thought about Dopey and his shovel. "Well," I said, "if they shot him—you know, in the head— I doubt the coroner will be able to tell, thanks to Brad's ham-fisted digging technique."

CeeCee looked at me. "You want to borrow my sweater?"

Surprised, I shook my head. "Why?"

"You're shivering."

I was, but not because I was cold.

"I'm okay," I said. "Look, CeeCee, it's really important you get them to run this story. And they have to do it soon. Like tomorrow."

She said, not looking up again from her notepad, "Oh, I know. And I think it'd go great alongside Dr. Clemmings's obituary, you know? The project he was working on when he died. That kind of thing."

"So," I said, "it'll run tomorrow? Do you think it'll run tomorrow?"

CeeCee shrugged. "They won't want to run it until they get the coroner's report on the body. And that could take weeks."

Weeks? I didn't have weeks. And though CeeCee didn't know it, she didn't have weeks either.

I was shaking uncontrollably now. Because I had realized, of course, what I'd just done: put CeeCee in the same kind of jeopardy I'd put Clive

Clemmings in. Clive had been just fine until Maria had overheard him telling his dictaphone what I'd said about Jesse. Then faster than you could say *The Haunting*, he was suffering from a massive, paranormally induced coronary. Had I just sentenced CeeCee to the same gruesome end? While I highly doubted Maria was going to ransack the offices of the *Carmel Pine Cone* the way she had the Carmel Historical Society, there was still a chance she might find out what I had done.

I needed that story to run right away. The sooner people found out the truth about Maria and Felix Diego, the better my chances of them not killing me—or the people I cared about.

"It's got to run tomorrow," I said. "Please, CeeCee. Can't you call the coroner and get some kind of unofficial statement?"

CeeCee did look up from her notebook then. She looked up and said, "Suze. What is the rush? These people have been dead for, like, forever. What does it matter?"

"It matters," I said. My teeth were starting to chatter. "It just really matters, okay, CeeCee? Please, *please* see what you can do to put a rush on it. And promise you won't talk about it. The story, I mean. Outside these offices. It's really important that you keep it to yourself."

CeeCee reached out and laid a hand on my bare shoulder. Her fingers were very warm and soft. "Suze," she said, peering down at me sort of intently. "What did you do to your head? Where'd that giant bruise under your bangs come from?"

I pushed self-consciously at my hair.

"Oh," I said. "I tripped. I fell into a hole. The hole they found the body in, isn't that funny?"

CeeCee didn't seem to think it was funny at all. She went, "Have you had a doctor look at that? Because it looks pretty bad. You might have a concussion, or something."

"I'm fine," I said, standing up. "Really. It's nothing. Look, I better go. Remember what I said, will you? About the story, I mean. It's really important that you don't mention it to anyone. And that you get them to run it as soon as possible. I need a lot of people to see it. A *lot* of people. They need to see the truth. You know. About the Diegos."

CeeCee stared at me. "Suze," she said. "Are you sure you're all right? I mean, since when do you care about the local gentry?"

I stammered, as I backed out of the cubicle, "Well, since meeting Dr. Clemmings, I guess. I mean, it's a real tragedy that people so often overlook their community's historical society, when you know, really, without it, the fabric of the—"

"You," CeeCee interrupted, "need to go home and take an Advil."

"You're right," I said, picking up my purse. It matched my slip dress, pink, with little flowers embroidered on it. I was overcompensating for all the days I'd had to wear those khaki shorts. "I'll go. See you later."

Then I got the hell out of there before my head exploded in front of everybody.

But on my way back to Father Dominic's car I realized that the reason I'd been shivering back in the photocopying cubicle hadn't been due to the excessive air-conditioning, the fact that Jesse was gone, or even the fact that two homicidal ghosts were actively trying to kill me.

No, I was shivering because of what I knew I was about to do.

When I got to Father Dom's car, I bent down and said through the open passenger window, "Hey."

Father Dominic started and hurled something out the driver's side window.

But it was too late. I'd already seen what he'd been up to. Plus I could smell it.

"Hey," I said again. "Give me one of those."

"Susannah." Father Dominic looked stern.

"Don't be ridiculous. Smoking is an awful habit. Believe me, you do not want to pick it up. How did things go with Miss Webb?"

"Um," I said. "Fine." I'm pretty sure it's a sin to tell a lie to a priest, even a white lie that can't possibly hurt him. But what was I supposed to do? I know him, see. And I know he's going to be completely rigid on the whole exorcism thing.

So what else could I do?

"She wants me to stick around, actually," I said, "and help her write it. The story, I mean."

Father Dominic's white eyebrows met over his silver frames. "Susannah," he said. "We have a great deal to do this afternoon, you and I—"

"Yeah," I said. "I know. But this is pretty important. How about I meet you back at your office at the Mission at five?"

Father Dominic hesitated. I could tell he thought I was up to something. Don't ask me how. I mean, I can be quite the angelic type, when I put my mind to it.

"Five o'clock," he said finally. "And not a minute later or, Susannah, I'm telling you right now, I will telephone your parents and tell them everything."

"Five o'clock," I said. "Promise."

I waved as he drove away, and then, just in case

he was looking in his rearview mirror, made as if to go back into the newspaper building.

But instead I slipped around the back of it, then headed toward the Pebble Beach Hotel and Golf Resort.

I had some unfinished business there.

chapter *thirteen*

He wasn't in the pool.

He wasn't eating burgers at the Pool House.

He wasn't on the tennis courts, at the stables, or in the pro shop.

Finally, I decided to check his room, although it didn't make any sense at all that he'd be there. Not on a gloriously sunny day like this one.

But when the door to his suite swung open to my knock, that's exactly where I found him. He was, Caitlin informed me tersely, taking a nap.

"Taking a nap?" I stared at her. "Caitlin, he's an eight-*year*-old, not an eight-*month*-old."

"He said he was tired," Caitlin snapped at me. "And what are you doing here, anyway? I thought you were supposed to be sick."

"I *am* sick," I said, pushing past her into the suite.

Caitlin eyed me disapprovingly. You could tell she was jealous of my slip dress and delicate pink sandals, not to mention my bag. I mean, compared to her, in her regulation Oxford T and pleated khakis, I looked like Gwyneth Paltrow. Only with better hair, of course.

"You don't look very sick to me," Caitlin declared.

"Oh, yeah?" I lifted up my bangs so she could see my forehead.

She sucked in her breath and made an oh-that-must-have-hurt face. "My God," she said. "How'd you do that?"

I thought about saying it was a job-related injury of some kind, so I could milk some disability out of her, but I didn't think it would work. Instead, I just said I'd tripped.

"So what are you doing here?" Caitlin wanted to know. "I mean, if you're not here to work."

"Well," I said. "That's the thing. I felt really guilty, you know, saddling you with Jack, so I got my mom to drop me off here after she took me to the doctor. I'll stay with him for the rest of the day, if you want."

Caitlin looked dubious. "I don't know," she said. "You're not in uniform—"

"Well, I wasn't going to wear my uniform to the *doctor's* office," I squealed. Really, it was amazing how these elaborate lies were tripping off my tongue. I could hardly believe it myself, and I was the one making them up. "I mean, come on. But look, he told me I'm fine, so there's no reason I can't take over for you. We'll just stay here in the suite, if you're that nervous about people seeing me out of uniform. No problem."

Caitlin glanced at my forehead again. "You're not on any kind of painkiller for that, are you? Because I can't have you babysitting all whacked up on Scooby Snacks."

I held up the first three fingers of my right hand in the international symbol for scouting.

"On my honor," I said, "I am not whacked up on Scooby Snacks."

Caitlin glanced at the closed door to Jack's room. "Well," she said hesitantly.

"Oh, come on," I said. "I could really use the dough. And don't you and Jake have a date tonight?"

Her gaze skittered toward me. "Well," she said, blushing.

Seriously. She *blushed*.

"Yeah," she said. "Actually, we do."

God. It had only been a guess.

"Don't you want to cut out a little early," I said, "to make yourself, you know, all glam for him?"

She giggled. Caitlin actually giggled. I am telling you, my stepbrothers ought to come with government warning labels: Caution, hazardous when mixed with estrogen.

"Okay," she said, and started heading for the door. "My boss'll kill me, though, if he sees you without your uniform, so you've got to stay in the room. Promise?"

I had made and broken so many promises in the past twenty-four hours, I didn't think one more could hurt. I went, "Sure thing, Caitlin."

And then I walked her to the door.

As soon as she was gone, I put down my purse and went into Jack's room. I did not knock first. There is nothing an eight-year-old boy's got that I haven't seen before. Besides, I was still a bit hacked with the little creep.

Jack may have been told to take a nap, but he certainly wasn't doing so. When I walked into his room, he thrust whatever it was he'd been playing with under the blankets and lifted his head from the pillow with his face all screwed up like he was sleepy.

Then he saw it was me, threw the covers back, and revealed that not only was he fully dressed, but that he'd been playing with his GameBoy.

"Suze!" he shouted, when he saw me. "You came back!"

"Yeah," I said. It was dark in his room. I went to the French doors and threw open the heavy drapes to let in the sunlight. "I came back."

"I thought," Jack said, jumping up and down excitedly on the bed, "that you were mad at me."

"I *am* mad at you," I said, turning around to look at him. The sight of that sparkling sea had dazzled my eyes, though, so I couldn't see him very well.

"What do you mean?" Jack stopped jumping. "What do you mean you're mad at me?"

Look, I wasn't going to screw around with the kid, okay? I just wish everyone had been as straight with me when I was his age. It is possible I wouldn't be so quick with my fists if I didn't have this pent-up inner rage from having been lied to so much as an eight-year-old. *Yes, Suze, of* course *there's really a Santa Claus,* but *No, there's no such thing as ghosts.* And then the clincher,

No, this shot I'm about to give you isn't going to hurt a bit.

"That ghost you exorcised?" I said, facing him with my hands on my hips. "He was my friend. My *best* friend."

I wasn't going to say boyfriend, or anything, because that wasn't true. But the hurt I was feeling must have shown in my voice, since Jack's lower lip started to jut out a little.

"What do you mean?" he wanted to know. "What do you mean, he was your friend? That's not what that lady said. The lady said—"

"That lady is a liar. That lady," I said, coming swiftly toward the bed and lifting up my bangs, "did *this* to me last night. See? Or at least, her husband did. All she tried to do was stab me with a knife."

Jack, standing on the bed, was taller than I was. He looked down at the bruise on my forehead with something like horror.

"Oh, Suze," he breathed. "Oh, Suze."

"You screwed up," I said to him, dropping my hand. "You didn't mean to. I understand that Maria tricked you. But you still screwed up, Jack."

Now his lower lip was trembling. So was his whole chin, actually. And his eyes had filled up with tears.

"I'm sorry, Suze," he said. His voice had gone about three pitches higher than usual. "Suze, I'm so sorry!"

He was trying really hard not to cry. He wasn't succeeding, though. Tears were spilling out of his eyes and rolling down his chubby cheeks . . . the only part of him that was chubby, except maybe for his Albert Einstein hair.

And even though I didn't want to, I found myself wrapping my arms around him and patting him on the back as he sobbed into my neck, telling him everything was going to be all right.

Just like, I realized, with something akin to horror, Father Dominic had done to me!

And just like him, I was completely lying. Because everything was *not* going to be all right. Not for me, at least. Not ever again. Unless I did something about it, and fast.

"Look," I said, after a few minutes of letting Jack wail. "Stop crying. We have work to do."

Jack lifted his head from my shoulder—which he had, by the way, gotten all wet with snot and tears and stuff, since my dress was sleeveless.

"What . . . what do you mean?" His eyes were red and squinty from crying. I was lucky nobody walked in right then. I definitely would have been convicted of child abuse or something.

"I'm going to try to get Jesse back," I explained, swinging Jack down from the bed. "And you're going to help me."

Jack went, "Who's Jesse?"

I explained. At least, I tried to. I told him that Jesse was the guy he had exorcised, and that he had been my friend, and that exorcising people was wrong, unless they'd done something very very bad, such as tried to kill you, which was, Jack explained, what Maria had told him Jesse'd tried to do to me.

So then I told Jack that ghosts are just like people; some of them are okay, but some of them are liars. If he had ever met Jesse, I assured him, he'd have known right away he was no killer.

Maria de Silva, on the other hand . . .

"But she seemed so nice," Jack said. "I mean, she's so pretty and everything."

Men. I'm serious. Even at the age of eight. It's pathetic.

"Jack," I said to him. "Have you ever heard the expression 'Don't judge a book by its cover?'"

Jack wrinkled his nose. "I don't like to read much."

"Well," I said. We had gone out into the living

room, and now I picked up my purse and opened it. "You're going to have to do some reading if we're going to get Jesse back. I'm going to need you to read this."

And I passed him an index card on which I'd scrawled some words. Jack squinted down at it.

"What is this?" he demanded. "This isn't English."

"No," I said. I started taking other things out of my purse. "It's Portuguese."

"What's that?" Jack asked.

"It's a language," I explained, "that they speak in Portugal. Also in Brazil, and a few other places."

"Oh," Jack said, then pointed at a small Tupperware container I'd taken from my purse. "What's *that*?"

"Oh," I said. "Chicken blood."

Jack made a face. "Eew!"

"Look," I said. "If we're going to do this exorcism, we're going to do it right. And to do it right, you need chicken blood."

Jack said, "I didn't use chicken blood when Maria was here."

"Yeah," I said. "Well, Maria does things her way, and I do things my way. Now let's go into the bathroom to do this. I have to paint stuff on the floor with the chicken blood, and I highly doubt the housekeeping staff will appreciate it if we do it here on the carpet."

Jack followed me into the bathroom that joined his room to his brother's. In the part of my brain that wasn't concentrating on what I was doing, I kind of wondered where Paul was. It was strange he hadn't called after that whole thing where he'd dropped me off at my house and there'd been all those cop cars and stuff in front of it. I mean, you'd have thought he'd wonder, at least, what that had been all about.

But I hadn't heard a peep out of him.

Not that I cared. I had way more important things to worry about. But it was still kind of odd.

"There," I said, when we had everything set up. It took an hour, but when we were done, we had a fairly decent example of how an exorcism—the Brazilian voodoo variety, anyway—is supposed to look. At least according to a book I'd read on the subject once.

With the chicken blood I'd procured from the meat counter of one of the gourmet shops downtown, I'd made these special symbols in the middle of the bathroom floor, and around them I'd stuck assorted candles (the votive kind, the only ones I could get at short notice, between the offices of the *Carmel Pine Cone* and the hotel; they were cinnamon scented, too, so the bathroom smelled sort of like Christmas . . . well, except for the not-so-festive fragrance of chicken blood).

In spite of the amateurishness with which it had been thrown together, it was, in fact, a working portal to the afterlife—or at least it would be, once Jack did his part with the notecard. I'd gone over the pronunciation of each word, and he seemed to have it down pretty well. The only thing he couldn't seem to get around was the fact that the person we were exorcising was, well, me.

"But you're *alive*," he kept saying. "If I exorcise your spirit from you, won't you be dead?"

Actually, this was a thought that had not really occurred to me. What *would* happen to my body after my spirit had left it? Would I be dead?

No, that was impossible. My heart and lungs wouldn't stop working just because my soul was gone. Probably I'd just lie there, like someone in a coma.

This was not, however, very comforting to Jack.

"But what if you don't come back?" he wanted to know.

"I'm going to come back," I said. "I told you. The only reason I *can* come back is that I do have a living body to return to. I just want to have a look around out there and see if Jesse's okay. If he is, fine. If not . . . well, I'll try to bring him back with me."

"But you just said the only reason you can come back is because you have a living body to return to. Jesse doesn't. So how can he come back?"

This was, of course, a good question. That was probably why it put me in such a bad mood.

"Look," I said finally. "Nobody has ever tried this before, so far as I know. Maybe you don't have to have a body to come back. I don't know, okay? But I can't not try just because I don't know the answer. Where would we be if Christopher Columbus hadn't tried? Huh?"

Jack looked thoughtful. "Living in Spain right now?"

"Very funny," I said. It was at this point that I took the last thing from my bag and tied one end around my waist. I tied the other end to Jack's wrist.

"What's the rope for?" he asked, looking down at it.

"So I can find my way back to you," I said.

Jack looked confused. "But if just your spirit's going, what's the point of tying a rope around your body? You said your body wasn't going anywhere."

"Jack," I said from between gritted teeth. "Just reel me back in if I'm gone more than half an hour, all right?" I figured half an hour was about as long as anybody's soul could be separated from their body. On TV I was always seeing stuff about little kids who'd slipped into icy water and drowned and been technically dead for up to forty minutes, yet recovered without any brain damage or anything. So I figured half an hour was cutting it as close as I could.

"But how—"

"Oh my God," I snapped at him. "Just do it, okay?"

Jack glowered at me. Hey, just because we're both mediators doesn't mean we get along all the time.

"Okay," he said. Under his breath, I heard him mutter, "You don't have to be such a witch about it."

Only he didn't say "witch." Really, it is shocking, the words kids are using these days.

"All right," I said. I stepped into the center of the circle of candles and stood in the middle of all the chicken blood symbols. "Here goes nothing."

Jack looked down at his notecard. Then he looked back up at me.

"Shouldn't you lie down?" he asked. "I mean, if it's gonna be like you're in a coma, I don't want you to fall down and hurt yourself."

He was right. I didn't want my hair to catch on fire or anything.

On the other hand, I didn't want to get chicken blood on my dress. I mean, it was an expensive one. Ninety-five dollars at Urban Outfitters.

Then I thought, *Suze, what is wrong with you? It's just a dress. You're doing this for Jesse. Isn't he worth more than ninety-five dollars?*

So I started to lie down.

But I had only managed to get down on one knee when there was a terrific thumping on the door to the suite.

I'll admit it. I panicked. I figured it was the fire department or somebody responding to to a report of smoke from someone whose bathroom vent adjoined Jack's.

"Quick," I hissed at him. "Blow out all the candles!"

236

While Jack hurried to do as I said, I stumbled to the door.

"Who is it?" I called sweetly when I got there.

"Susannah," an all-too-familiar voice said. "Open the door this instant."

chapter *fourteen*

If you ask me, Father D. way overreacted.

I mean, first of all, I had the situation completely under control.

And second, it wasn't as if we'd sacrificed any small animals, or whatever. I mean, the chicken had already been dead.

So all that stomping around and calling us names was really unnecessary.

Not that he called Jack any names. No, most of the names were hurled at me. Apparently, if I am intent on destroying myself, that is one thing. But to force a small boy to aid in my self-destruction? That is just despicable.

And my pointing out that the small boy was the

one who'd created the need for me to behave self-destructively? Yeah, that didn't go over too well.

But what the whole thing did do was illustrate to Father Dominic just how serious I was about my plan. I guess it finally got through to him that I was going to do my best to find Jesse, with or without his help.

So he decided that, under those circumstances, he had better help, if only to improve my chances of not hurting myself, or anybody else.

"It will not," he said, looking all tight-lipped about it as he unlocked the doors to the basilica, "be any fly-by-night operation either. None of this Brazilian voodoo business. We are going to perform a decent Christian exorcism, or none at all."

Really, if you think about it, I probably have the most bizarre conversations of anyone on the planet. Seriously. I mean, a *decent Christian exorcism*?

But it isn't just the conversations I have that are bizarre. I mean, the circumstances under which I have them are pretty bizarre, too. For instance, I was having this one in a dark empty church. Dark because it was after midnight, and empty for the same reason.

"And you are going to have adult supervision," Father Dominic went on as he ushered me inside.

"How you could have expected that boy to successfully perform so complicated a procedure, I simply cannot imagine. . . ."

He had been ranting in that particular vein all afternoon. All the way up until Jack's parents—not to mention Paul—had gotten back to the suite, as a matter of fact. Father D. hadn't, of course, been able to whisk me off right away the way he'd wanted to, because of Jack. Instead, Jack and I had been forced to clean up the mess we'd made—it is no joke sponging chicken blood out from between bathroom tiles, let me tell you—and then we'd had to sit and wait for Dr. and Mrs. Slater to return from their tennis lesson. Jack's parents had looked a little surprised to find the three of us sitting there on the couch. I mean, think about it: a babysitter, a boy, and a priest? Talk about feeling as if you were whacked up on Scooby Snacks.

But what was I supposed to do? Father D. wouldn't leave without me. He didn't trust me not to try exorcising myself.

So the three of us sat there while Father D. lectured us on the fine art of mediation. He talked for two hours. I'm not kidding. *Two hours*. I can tell you, Jack was probably regretting ever having told me about the whole I-see-dead-people thing by the end of it. He was probably all, *Uh, yeah, about the dead people? Joking, guys. I was joking. . . .*

But I don't know, maybe it was good the little guy got the dos and don'ts. God knew I hadn't been too lucid with my own Intro to Mediation. I mean, if I'd been a little clearer on the finer points, maybe this whole thing with Jesse would never have—

But whatever. You can only beat yourself up so much. I was fully aware the entire mess was my own fault. That's why I was so intent on fixing it.

Oh, and the part about my being in love with the guy? Yeah, that had a little something to do with it, too.

Anyway, that's what we were doing when Jack's parents walked in: listening to Father D. drone on about responsibility and courtesy when dealing with the undead.

Father Dominic dried up when Dr. and Mrs. Slater, followed by Paul, came into the suite. They, in turn, stopped chatting about their dinner plans and just stood there, staring.

Paul was the one who came out of it first.

"Suze," he said, smiling. "What a surprise. I thought you weren't feeling well."

"I recovered," I said, standing up. "Dr. and Mrs. Slater, Paul, this is, um, the principal of my school,

Father Dominic. He was nice enough to give me a ride over so that I could, um, visit Jack. . . ."

"How do you do?" Father Dominic got quickly to his feet. Like I said, Father D.'s no slouch in the looks department. He cut a pretty impressive figure, all snowy-topped six feet of him. He didn't look like the kind of guy you'd feel funny about finding in your hotel suite with your eight-year-old and his babysitter, which is saying quite a lot, you know.

When Dr. and Mrs. S heard that Father D. was affiliated with the Junipero Serra Mission, they got all chummy and started saying how they'd been on the tour, and how impressive it was and all. I guess they didn't want him to think they were the kind of people who came to a town with a historically significant slice of Americana attached to it, and then spent the whole time they were there playing golf and downing mimosas.

While his parents and Father D. schmoozed, Paul sidled up to me and whispered, "What are you doing tonight?"

I thought about telling him the truth: "Oh, nothing. Just having my soul exorcised so I can roam around purgatory, looking for the ghost of the dead cowboy who used to live in my bedroom."

But that, you know, might have sounded flippant, or like one of those made-up excuses girls use. You know, the old "I'm washing my hair" put-down. So I just said, "I've got plans."

Paul went, "Too bad. I was hoping we could take a drive up to Big Sur and watch the sunset, then maybe grab something to eat."

"Sorry," I said with a smile. "Sounds great, but like I said, I've got plans."

Most guys would have dropped it after that, but Paul, for some reason, did not. He even reached out and casually draped an arm around my shoulders . . . if you can do something like that casually. Somehow, though, he pulled it off. Maybe because he's from Seattle.

"Suze," he said, dipping his voice low, so that no one else in the room could overhear him—especially his little brother, who was clearly straining his neck in an effort to do so. "It's Friday night. We're leaving day after tomorrow. You and I might never see each other again. Come on. Throw a guy a bone, will you?"

I don't have guys pursuing me all that often—at least, not hotties like Paul. I mean, most of the guys who've liked me since I moved to California . . . well, there've been some serious relationship issues, such as the fact that they ended up serving long prison terms for murder.

So this was pretty new for me. I was impressed in spite of myself.

Still, I'm not a dope. Even if I hadn't been in love with somebody else, Paul Slater was from out of town. It's easy for guys who are leaving in a couple of days to give a girl the rush. I mean, come on: They don't have to commit.

"Gosh," I said. "That is just so sweet. But you know what? I really do have other plans." I stepped out from beneath his arm and totally interrupted Dr. Slater's in-depth description of that day's golf score—bogey, bogey, par, par. "Can you give me a lift home, Father D.?"

Father Dominic said he could, of course, and we left. I noticed Paul giving me the old hairy eyeball as we said our good-byes, but I figured it was because he was hacked at me for turning down his dinner invitation.

I didn't know it was for entirely different reasons. At least, not then. Although, of course, I should have. I really should have.

Anyway, Father D. lectured me all the way home. He was way mad, madder than he'd ever been with me before, and I've done some stuff that's gotten him plenty peeved. I wanted to know how he'd figured out I was at the hotel and not back at the paper helping CeeCee write her story, like I'd said I'd be, and he said it hadn't been hard: He just remembered that CeeCee was a straight-A student who surely wouldn't need *my* help writing anything, and turned his car around. When he found out I'd left ten minutes earlier, he tried to think where he would have gone under similar circumstances, back when he was my age.

"The hotel was the obvious choice," Father Dominic informed me as we pulled up in front of my house. No ambulances this time, I was relieved to note. Just the shady pine trees and the tinny sound of the radio Andy was listening to in the backyard as he worked on the deck. A sleepy summer evening. Not at all the kind of night you'd think of when you heard the word *exorcism*.

"You are not," Father D. went on, "precisely unpredictable, Susannah."

Predictable I may be, but it has apparently worked to my advantage, since right before I got out of the car, Father D. went, "I'll return at midnight to bring you down to the Mission."

I looked at him in surprise. "The Mission?"

"If we're going to perform an exorcism," he said tersely, "we're going to do it correctly, in a house of the Lord. Unfortunately, the monsignor, as you know, is sure to frown on such a use of church property, so while I dislike having to resort to subterfuge, I can see that you will not be swayed from this course, and so it will unfortunately be necessary in this case. I want to make certain there's no chance of Sister Ernestine or anyone else discovering us. Therefore, midnight it will have to be."

And midnight, therefore, it was.

I can't really tell you what I did in the meantime. I was too nervous, really, to do much of anything. We had takeout for dinner. I don't know what it was. I hardly tasted it. It was just me and my mom and Andy, since Sleepy had a date with Caitlin, and Dopey was with his latest skank.

The only thing I know for sure is that CeeCee called with the news that the story on the dysfunctional de Silva/Diego family was going to run in the Sunday edition of the paper.

"It'll reach thirty-five thousand people," CeeCee assured me. "Way more than our circulation during the week. More people subscribe to the Sunday paper because of the funnies and all."

The coroner, she informed me, had come through with a tentative confirmation of my story: The skeleton found in my backyard was between one hundred and fifty to one hundred and seventy-five years old, and belonged to a male of twenty to twenty-five years of age.

"Race," CeeCee went on, "is difficult to determine due to the damage to the skull from Brad's shovel. But they were certain about the cause of death."

I clutched the receiver to my ear, conscious that my mother and Andy, over at the dinner table, could hear every word.

"Oh?" I said, trying to keep my tone light. But I could feel myself getting cold again, just like I had that afternoon in the photocopy cubicle.

"Asphyxiation," CeeCee said. "There's like some bone in the neck they can tell by."

"So he was . . . "

"Strangled," CeeCee said matter-of-factly. "Hey, what are you doing tonight, anyway? Wanna hang? Adam's got some family thing he has to go to. We could rent a movie—"

"No," I said. "No, I can't. Thanks, CeeCee. Thanks a lot."

I hung up the phone.

Strangled. Jesse had died from being strangled. By Felix Diego. Funny, I had somehow always figured he'd been shot to death. But strangling made more sense: People would have heard a shot and come to investigate. Then there'd have been no question about what happened to Hector de Silva.

But strangling someone? That was pretty much silent. Felix could easily have strangled Jesse in his sleep, then carried his dead body into the backyard and then buried it, along with his belongings. No one would have been the wiser. . . .

I guess I must have stood there looking down at the phone for a while, since my mom went, "Suze? Are you all right, honey?"

I jumped and went, "Yeah, Mom. Sure. I'm fine."

But I hadn't been fine then. And I certainly wasn't fine now.

I had only been to the Mission after dark a couple times before, and it was still as creepy now as it had been then . . . long shadows, dark recesses, spooky noises as our footsteps echoed down the aisle between the pews. There was this statue of the Virgin Mary right by the doorway, and Adam had told me once that if you walked by it while thinking an impure thought, the statue would weep blood.

Well, my thoughts as I walked into the basilica weren't exactly impure, but I noticed as I passed the Virgin Mary that she looked more particularly prone to weeping blood than usual. Or maybe it was just the dark.

In any case, I was creeped out. Above my head yawned the huge dome you could see, glowing red in the sun and blue in the moon, from my bedroom window, while before me loomed the chancel in which the altar glowed, swathed in white.

Father Dom had been busy, I saw when I entered the church. Candles had been set up in a wide circle just before the altar rail. Father Dominic, still muttering to himself about my need for adult supervision, stooped down and began lighting the wicks.

"That's where you're—I mean, we're—going to do it?" I asked.

Father Dominic straightened and surveyed his handiwork.

"Yes," he said. Then, misreading my expression, he added dourly, "Don't let the absence of chicken blood fool you, Susannah. I assure you the Catholic exorcism ceremony is highly effective."

"No," I said quickly. "It's just that . . ."

I looked at the floor in the middle of the circle of candles. The floor looked very hard—way harder than the bathroom floor back at the hotel. That was tile. This was marble. Remembering what Jack had said, I went, "What if I fall down? I might conk my head again."

"Fortunately, you will be lying down," Father D. said.

"Can't I have a pillow or something?" I asked. "I mean, come on. That floor looks cold." I glanced at the altar cloth. "How about that? Can I lie on that?"

Father Dominic looked pretty shocked for a guy who was about to exorcise a girl who was neither possessed nor dead.

"For goodness' sake, Susannah," he said. "That would be sacrilegious."

Instead he went and got some choir robes for me. I made a nice little bed on the floor between all the candles, then lay down on it. It was actually quite comfortable.

Too bad my heart was pounding way too hard for me ever to have been able to doze off.

"All right, Susannah," Father D. said. He wasn't happy with me. He hadn't been happy with me, I knew, for some time. But he was bowing to the inevitable.

Still, he seemed to feel one last lecture was necessary.

"I am willing to help you with this ridiculous scheme of yours, but only because I realize that if I do not, you will try to do it on your own, or with, God forbid, that boy's help." Father D. was looking at me very sternly from where he stood. "But do not think for one minute that I approve."

I opened my mouth to argue, but Father Dominic held up one hand.

"No," he said. "Allow me to finish, please. What Maria de Silva did was wrong, and I realize you are only trying to correct that wrong. But I am afraid I cannot see any of this ending happily. It is my experience, Susannah—and I hope you will agree that my experience is significantly greater than yours—that once spirits are exorcised, they stay that way."

Again I opened my mouth, and again Father D. shushed me.

"Where you are going," he went on, "will be like a waiting area for spirits who have passed from the astral plane but have not yet reached their final destination. If Jesse is still there, and you manage to find him—and you understand that I consider this a very great if, because I don't think you're going to—do not be surprised if he chooses to stay where he is."

"Father D.," I began, rising up onto my elbows, but he shook his head.

"It might be his only chance, Susannah," Father Dominic said somberly, "of ever moving on."

"No," I said. "That's not true. There's a reason, see, that he's hung around my house for so long. All he has to do is figure out what that reason is, and he'll be able to move on on his own—"

"Susannah," Father Dominic interrupted. "I'm sure it isn't that simple—"

"He has a right," I insisted through gritted teeth, "to decide for himself."

"I agree," Father Dominic said. "That's what I'm trying to say, Susannah. If you find him, you must let him decide. And you mustn't . . . well, you mustn't attempt to use any sort of, er . . ."

I just blinked up at him. "Father D.," I said. "What are you talking about?"

"Well, it's only that . . ." Father Dominic looked more embarrassed than I had ever seen him. I could not, for the life of me, figure out what was wrong with him. "I see that you changed . . ."

I looked down at myself. I had changed out of my pink slip dress and into a black one that had little red rosebuds embroidered on it. This I had paired with some totally cute Prada slides. I had had a hard enough time choosing an ensemble. I mean, what do you wear to an exorcism? I totally did not need Father D. dissing my duds.

"What?" I demanded defensively. "What's wrong with it? Too funereal? It's too funereal, isn't it? I *knew* black was all wrong for the occasion."

"Nothing's wrong with it," Father Dominic said. "It's simply that . . . Susannah, you mustn't attempt to use your, um, sexual wiles to influence Jesse's decision."

My mouth dropped open. Okay. Now I was mad.

"Father Dominic!" I sat up and yelled. After that, though, I was completely speechless. I couldn't think of anything to say except, "As if!"

"Susannah," Father Dominic said severely. "Don't pretend you don't know what I mean. I know you care about Jesse. All I'm asking is that you don't use your"—he cleared his throat—"feminine charms to manipulate his—"

"Like I *could*," I grumbled.

"Yes." Father Dominic's tone was firm. "You could. All I'm asking is that you don't. For the good of both of you. *Don't.*"

"Fine," I said. "I won't. I wasn't planning to."

"I'm delighted to hear that," Father Dominic said. He opened a small, leather-bound book and began flipping through the pages. "Shall we begin, then?"

"I suppose." Still grumbling, I lay back down. I couldn't believe Father D. had just suggested what he had—that I would use my sex appeal to lure Jesse back to me. Ha! Father D. was overlooking two simple things: one being that I'm not so sure I have sex appeal, and two, that if I do, Jesse had certainly never noticed.

Still, Father Dominic had felt obliged to say something about it, which must mean he'd noticed something. Must be the dress. Not bad for $59.95.

As I lay there, a slow grin crept over my face. Father D. had used the word *sexual*. About *me*!

Excellent.

Father D. began reading from his little book. As he read, he swung this metal ball that had smoke coming out of it. The smoke was from the incense burning inside the metal ball. Let me tell you, it stank.

I couldn't understand what Father D. was saying, since it was all in Latin. It sounded nice, though. I lay there in my black slip dress and wondered if I ought to have worn pants. I mean, who knew what I was going to find up there? What if I had to do some climbing? People might see my underwear.

You would have thought I'd be pondering more profound thoughts than this, but I am very sorry to report that the deepest thing I thought about while Father Dominic was exorcising my soul was that when this was all over, and Jesse was home, and Maria and Felix had been locked back up in their crypt where they belonged, I was going to have to take a really long soak in that hot tub Andy was installing, because let me tell you, I was *sore*.

And then something started happening above my head. A section of the domed ceiling disappeared and was replaced by all this smoke. Then I realized it was the smoke from the incense Father D. was waving around. It was curling like a tornado above my head.

Then, in the center of the tornado, I saw the night sky. Really. Like the dome over the top of the basilica wasn't there anymore. I could see stars twinkling coldly. I didn't recognize any constellations, even though Jesse had been trying to teach them to me. Back in Brooklyn, you couldn't see the stars so well because of the city lights. So other than the Big Dipper, which you can always see, I don't know the names of any of the constellations.

It didn't matter. This wasn't the sky I was seeing. Not Earth's sky, anyway. It was something else. Someplace else.

"Susannah," Father Dominic said gently.

I started, then looked at him. I had been, I realized, half asleep, staring up at that sky.

"What?" I asked.

"It's time," Father Dominic said.

chapter *fifteen*

Father Dominic looks funny, I thought. *Why does he look so funny?*

I realized why when I sat up. That's because only part of me sat up. The rest of me stayed where I was, lying on the choir robes with my eyes closed.

You know on *Sabrina the Teenage Witch* when she splits into two people, so one can go to the party with Harvey and the other can go to the witch convention with her aunts? That's what had happened to me. I was two people now.

Except that only one of them was conscious. The other half was just lying there with her eyes closed. And you know what? That bruise on my forehead really did look disgusting. No wonder everyone who saw it recoiled in horror.

"Susannah," Father Dominic said. "Are you all right?"

I tore my gaze from my unconscious self.

"Fine," I said. I looked down at my spiritual self, which appeared to me to be exactly the same as the person beneath me, except that I was glowing a little. An excellent fashion accessory, by the way, if you can get it. You know, that all-over spectral glow can really do things for a girl's complexion.

Plus something else. The bruise on my forehead? Yeah, it didn't hurt anymore.

"You don't have much time," Father Dominic said. "Just half an hour."

I blinked at him. "How am I supposed to know when half an hour is up? I don't have a watch." I don't wear one because somehow they always end up getting smashed by some recalcitrant spirit. Besides, who wants to know what time it is? The news is almost always disappointing.

"Wear mine," Father Dom said, and he took off his enormous steel-link man watch and gave it to me.

It was the first object I picked up in my new ghostly state. It felt absurdly heavy. Still, I managed to fasten it around my wrist, where it jangled loosely, like a bracelet. Or a prison shackle.

"Okay," I said, looking up at that hole above me. "Here goes nothing."

I had to climb, of course. Don't ask me why I hadn't thought of this. I mean, I had to reach up and grab the edges of that hole in time and space and boost myself up into it. And in a slip dress, no less.

Whatever. I was about halfway in when I heard a familiar voice shriek my name.

Father Dominic spun around. I leaned down from the hole—through which I could only see fog, gray fog that spritzed my face damply—and saw Jack, of all people, running down the church aisle toward us, his pale face white with fear, and something trailing behind him.

Father Dominic reached out and caught him just before he flung himself on my unconscious form. He obviously didn't see my legs dangling from the enormous tear in the church ceiling.

"What are you doing here?" Father Dominic demanded, his face almost as white as the kid's. "Do you have any idea what time it is? Do your parents know you're here? They must be worried sick—"

"They're—they're asleep," Jack panted. "Please, Suze forgot . . . she forgot her rope." Jack held up the long white object that had been skittering along behind him as he'd run between the pews. It was my rope from our first attempt to exorcise me. "How is she going to find her way back without her rope?"

Father Dominic took the rope from Jack without a word of thanks. "It was very wrong of you, Jack," he said disapprovingly, "to come here. What could you have been thinking? I told you it was going to be very dangerous."

"But . . . " Jack kept looking at my unconscious half. "Her rope. She forgot her rope."

"Here," I called, from my celestial hole. "Toss it up here."

Jack looked up at me, and the anxiety left his face.

"Suze!" he yelled delightedly. "You're a ghost!"

"Shhh!" Father Dominic looked pained. "Really, young man, you must keep your voice down."

"Hi, Jack," I said from my hole. "Thanks for bringing the rope. How'd you get down here, anyway?"

"Hotel shuttle," Jack said proudly. "I snuck onto it. It was coming into town to pick up a lot of drunk people. When it stopped near the Mission, I snuck off."

I couldn't have been prouder if he'd been my own son. "Good thinking," I said.

"This," Father Dominic moaned, "is the last thing we need right now. Here, Susannah, take the rope, and for the love of God, hurry—"

I leaned down and grabbed the end of the rope, then tied it securely around my waist. "Okay," I said. "If I'm not back in half an hour, start pulling."

"Twenty-five minutes," Father Dominic corrected me. "We lost time, thanks to this young man's interruption." He took a pocket watch from his coat with the hand that wasn't clutching the other end of the rope. "Go now, Susannah," he urged me.

"Right," I said. "Okay. Be right back."

And then I swung my legs into the hole. When I looked down, I could see Father Dominic and Jack standing there, peering up at me. And I could also see me, asleep like Snow White, in a circle of dancing candle flames. Although I doubt Snow White ever wore Prada.

I got up and looked around me. Nothing.

I'm serious. There was nothing there. Just that black sky, through which a few stars burned coldly. And then there was the fog. Thick, ever-moving, cool fog. *I should have*, I thought to myself with a shiver, *worn a sweater*. The fog seemed to weigh down the air I was taking into my lungs. It also seemed to serve as a muffler. I couldn't hear a sound, not even my own footsteps.

Oh, well. Twenty-five minutes wasn't long. I sucked in a chestful of damp air and yelled, "Jesse!"

It was a highly effective move. Not that Jesse showed up. Oh, no. But this other guy did.

In a gladiator outfit, no less.

I'm not even kidding. He looked like the guy from my mom's American Express card (which I frequently borrow—with her permission, of course). You know, the broom sticking out of his helmet, the leather miniskirt, the big sword. I couldn't see his feet on account of the fog, but I assumed that, if I could, he'd be wearing lace-up sandals (so unflattering on people with fat knees).

"You," he said in this deep, no-nonsense voice, "do not belong here."

See. I knew the slip dress had been a mistake. But who knew purgatory had a dress code?

"I know," I said, giving him my best smile. Maybe Father D. was right. Maybe I do have a tendency to use my sexuality to get what I want. I was certainly laying on the girlie thing thick for the Russell Crowe type in front of me.

"The thing is," I said, fingering my rope. "I'm looking for a friend. Maybe you know him. Jesse de Silva? He showed up here last night, I think. He's about twenty, six feet tall, black hair, dark eyes—" Killer abs?

Russell Crowe must not have been listening closely, since all he said was, "You do not belong here," again.

Okay, the slip dress had definitely been a mistake. Because how was I supposed to kick this guy out of my way without splitting the skirt?

"Look, mister," I said, striding up to him and trying not to notice that his pectoral muscles were so pronounced, that his breasts were bigger than mine. Way bigger. "I told you. I'm looking for someone. Now either you tell me if you've seen him, or you get out of my face, okay? I'm a mediator, all right? I have just as much right to be here as you."

I did not, of course, know if this was true, but heck, I've been a mediator all my life, and I haven't gotten squat for it. As far as I was concerned, somebody owed me, but big.

The gladiator seemed to agree. He went, in a completely different tone, "A mediator?" He looked down at me as if I were a monkey that had suddenly sat up and started saying the Pledge of Allegiance.

Still, I must have done something right, since he said slowly, "I know the one of whom you speak."

Then he seemed to come to a decision. Stepping to one side, he said in a commanding voice, "Go now. Do not open any doors. He will come."

I stared at him. Whoa. "Are you . . . are you serious?"

For the first time, he showed some personality. He went, "Do I seem to be joking to you?"

"Um," I said. "No."

"Because I am the gatekeeper. I do not joke. Go now." He pointed. "You have not much time."

Off in the distance, in the direction he was pointing, I saw something. I don't know what it was, but it was something other than fog. I felt like hugging my new gladiator friend, but I restrained myself. He didn't seem the touchy-feely sort.

"Thanks," I said. "Thanks a whole lot."

"Hurry," the gatekeeper said. "And remember, whatever you do, do not go toward the light."

I had given the rope a yank so that Father D. would give me some slack. Now I just stood there with it in my hands, staring at the gladiator.

"Don't go into the light?" I echoed. "You're not serious."

I swear to you, he sounded indignant. "I told you before, I do not joke. Why do you think I would say something I do not mean?"

I wanted to tell him that the whole don't-go-into-the-light thing was way overplayed. I mean, *Poltergeist* one through three had pretty much run that line into the ground.

But who knew? Maybe the guy who wrote those movies was a mediator. Maybe he and the gatekeeper were pals or something.

"Okay," I said, sidling past him. "Gotcha. Don't go into the light."

"Or open any doors," the gatekeeper reminded me.

"No doors," I said, pointing at him and winking. "You got it."

Then I turned around, and the fog was gone.

Well, not gone, really. I mean, it was still there, licking at my heels. But most of it had given way, so that I could see I was in a corridor lined with doors. There was no ceiling overhead, just those coldly winking stars and inky black sky. Still, the long corridor of closed doors seemed to stretch out forever before me.

And I wasn't supposed to open any of those doors. Or go into the light.

Well, the second part was easy. I didn't see any light to go toward. But how was I not supposed to open one of those doors? I mean, really. What was going on behind them? What would I find if I opened one, just a crack, and peeked in? Alternate universe? The planet Vulcan? Maybe a world where Suze Simon was a normal girl, not a mediator? Maybe one where Suze Simon was homecoming queen and the most popular person in the whole school, and Jesse wasn't a ghost and could actually take her to dances and had his own car and didn't live in her bedroom?

Then I stopped wondering what was behind all those doors. That's because coming down the hallway toward me—as if he'd just materialized there from out of nowhere—came Jesse.

He looked pretty surprised to see me. I don't know if it was the fact that I was standing there in what was, I suppose, heaven's waiting room, or if it was the attractive length of cord around my waist, which did not, I have to admit, go with the rest of my outfit.

Whatever it was, he looked pretty shocked.

"Oh," I said, reaching up to make sure my bangs were covering my unsightly bruise. "Hi."

Jesse froze in his tracks and just stared at me. It was like he couldn't believe what he was seeing. He didn't look any different from the last time I'd seen him. I mean, the last time I'd seen his ghost. The last time I'd seen him, of course, it had been a view of his rotten corpse, and the sight had, of course, made me lose my supper.

But this Jesse was a lot easier on the eyes.

Still, if I'd expected any sort of joyful reunion— a hug or, God forbid, a kiss—I was in for a disappointment. He just stood there, staring at me like I'd grown two heads since the last time we'd bumped into each other.

"Susannah," he breathed. "What are you doing here? Are you—you're not—"

I caught his meaning at once and went, with a nervous laugh, "Dead? Me? No, no, no. No. I just, um, I came up here because I wanted to, um, you know, see if you were all right. . . ."

Okay, could I be any lamer? I mean, seriously. I had pictured this moment in my head a thousand times since I'd first decided I was going to come after him, and in all my fantasies, no explanations were ever necessary. Jesse just threw his arms around me and started kissing me. On the lips.

This, though. This was way awkward. I wished I'd prepared a speech.

"Um," I said. What I really wished was that I could stop saying *um*. "See, the thing is, I wanted to make sure you were here because you wanted to be. Because if you don't want to be, well, Father Dom and I thought maybe it would be possible for you to come back. To, um, finish whatever it is, you know, that was keeping you down there. In my world, I mean. Our world," I corrected myself, quickly, remembering Father Dominic's warning. "Our world, I mean."

Jesse continued to just stare at me.

"Susannah," he said. His voice sounded weird. I figured out why a second later, when he asked, "Weren't you the one who sent me here?"

I gaped at him. "What? What are you talking about?"

Now I knew what was so weird about his voice. It was filled with hurt. "Didn't you," he asked, "have me exorcised?"

"Me?" My own voice rocketed up about ten octaves. "*Me?* Jesse, of course not. I would never do that. I mean, you know I would never do something like that. That kid Jack did it. Your girlfriend Maria made him do it. She was trying to get rid of you. She told Jack you were bothering me, and he didn't know any better, so he exorcised you, and then Felix Diego threw me off the porch roof, and Jesse, they found your body, I mean your bones, and I saw them and I threw up all over the side of the house, and Spike really misses you and I was just thinking, you know, if you wanted to come back, you could, because that's why I've got this rope, so we can find our way back."

I was babbling. I have a tendency to do this even when I am not standing in purgatory. But I couldn't help myself. Everything was just kind of spilling out. Well, not everything. I mean, I totally wasn't going to tell him *why* I wanted him to come back. I wasn't going to mention the L word or anything. And not even because of Father D.'s warning, either.

"That is," I went on, "if you want to come back. I could see why you'd want to stay here. I mean, after a hundred and fifty years and all, it's probably a relief. I imagine they'll be moving you along soon, and you'll be getting a new life, or going up to heaven, or whatever. But I was just thinking, you know, it wasn't fair of Maria to do what she did to you—twice—and that if you want to come back and figure out what it was you were, you know, doing down there on earth for so long, well, I'd just give you a hand, if I could."

I looked down at Father D.'s watch. It was easier

than looking into Jesse's face, and seeing that he still wore that inscrutable expression, as if he couldn't quite believe what he was seeing. And hearing.

"The only thing is," I said, "I can be separated from my body for half an hour before I wind up permanently detached, and we only have fifteen minutes left. So you have to hurry up and decide. What's it going to be?"

Was that, I wondered, *unfeminine enough for Father Dom?* I was so totally not working it. No one could accuse me even of *smiling*. I was the picture of a professional mediator.

Only I didn't know how long I was going to be able to maintain my businesslike persona. Especially when Jesse reached out, like he did just then, and laid a hand on my arm.

"Susannah," he said, and now his voice wasn't filled with hurt at all, but something that, if I wasn't mistaken, sounded a lot like anger. "Are you saying you *died* for me?"

"Um," I said, wondering if it would count as using my feminine wiles if *he* was the one who touched *me*. "Well, not technically. Yet. But if we hang around here much longer—"

The hand on my arm tightened. "Let's go," he said.

I wasn't sure he really understood the situation. "Jesse," I said. "I can find my own way back, okay? I'm like this with the gatekeeper." I held up crossed fingers. "If you want to come with me because you want to go back, that's fine, but if you just want to walk me back to my hole, believe me, I can get there on my own."

Jesse just said, "Susannah. Shut up."

And then, still keeping one hand on my arm, he grabbed the rope and started following it, back in the direction from which I'd come.

Oh, I thought as he propelled me along. Okay. Great. Now he's mad at me. Here I risk my life—because let's face it, that's what I was doing—and he's *mad* at me because of it. I actually should have thought of this. I mean, risking your life for a guy is practically like using the L word. Worse, even. How was I going to get out of this one?

I said, "Jesse, don't flatter yourself that I did this for you. I mean, it has been nothing but one giant pain in the neck, having you for a roommate. Do you think I like having to come home from school or from work or whatever and having to explain stuff like the Bay of Pigs to you? Believe me, life with you is no picnic."

He didn't say anything. He just kept pulling me along.

"Or what about Tad?" I said, bringing up what I knew was a sore subject. "I mean, you think I like having you tag along on my dates? Having you out of my life is going to make things a lot simpler, so don't think, you know, I did this for you. I only did it because that stupid cat of yours has been crying its head off. And also because anything I can do to make your stupid girlfriend mad, I will."

"*Nombre de Dios*, Susannah," Jesse muttered. "Maria's not my girlfriend."

"Well, she certainly used to be," I said. "And what about that, anyway? That girl is a full-on skank, Jesse. I can't believe you ever agreed to marry her. I mean, what were you thinking, anyway? Couldn't you see what she was like underneath all that lace?"

"Things," Jesse said through gritted teeth, "were different back then, Susannah."

"Oh, yeah? So different that you couldn't tell the girl you were about to marry was a big old—"

"I hardly knew her," Jesse said, hauling me to a stop and glaring down at me. "All right?"

"Nice try," I said. "You two were cousins. Which is a whole other issue which, if you really want to know, completely grosses me—"

"Yes, we were cousins," Jesse interrupted, giving

my arm a shake. "But like I said before, things were different back then, Susannah. If we had more time, I'd tell you—"

"Oh, no, you don't. We still have"—I looked down at Father D's watch—"twelve minutes left. You tell me now."

"Susannah—"

"*Now*, Jesse, or I swear, I'm not budging."

He actually groaned in frustration, and said what I think must have been a very bad word, only I don't know for sure, since it was in Spanish. They don't teach us swears in Spanish at school.

"Fine," he said, dropping my arm. "You want to know? You want to know how it was back then? It was different, all right? California was different. Completely different. There was none of this mingling of the sexes. Boys and girls did not play together, did not sit side by side in classrooms. The only time I was ever in the same room with Maria was at meals, or sometimes dances. And then we were surrounded by other people. I doubt I ever heard her speak more than a few words—"

"Well, they were evidently pretty impressive ones, since you agreed to marry her."

Jesse ran a hand through his hair and made

another other exclamation in Spanish. "Of course I agreed to marry her," he said. "My father wanted it, her father wanted it. How could I say no? I didn't want to say no. I didn't know—not then—what she was. It was only later, when I got her letters, that I realized—"

"That she can't spell?"

He ignored me. "—that the two of us had nothing in common, and never would. But even then, I would not have disgraced my family by breaking things off with her. Not for that."

"But when you heard she wasn't as pure as the driven snow?" I folded my arms across my chest and glared at him, sexist product of the nineteenth century that he was. "That's when you decided she wasn't good wife material?"

"When I heard rumors about Maria and Felix Diego," he said impatiently, "I was unhappy. I knew Diego. He was not a good man. He was cruel and . . . Well, he was always looking for ways to make money. And Maria had a lot of money. He wanted to marry her—you can guess why—so when I found out, I decided it might be better to end it, yes—"

"But Diego got to know you first," I said, a throb in my voice.

"Susannah." He stared down at me. "I've had a

century and a half to get used to being dead. It no longer matters to me who killed me, or why. What's important to me right now is seeing that you do not end up the same way. Now will you move, or do I have to carry you?"

"Okay," I said, letting him pull me along again. "But I just want to get one thing straight. I did not do all this—you know, get myself exorcised and come up here and all—because I'm in love with you or anything like that."

"I would not," he said grimly, "as you say, flatter myself."

"Damn straight," I said. I wondered if I was still being unfeminine enough. Actually, I was beginning to think I was being a little *too* unfeminine. Hostile, actually, was what I was being. "Because I'm not. I came because of the cat. The cat really misses you."

"You shouldn't have come at all," Jesse said under his breath. Still, I heard him, anyway. It wasn't like there was a whole lot of other noise up there. We had left the corridor—it had disappeared, I saw, the minute we turned our backs to it—and were back in the fog again, following the rope that, thankfully, Jack had remembered. "I cannot believe that Father Dominic allowed it."

"Hey," I said. "Leave Father D. out of it. This is

all your fault, you know. None of this would have happened if you had just been open and honest with me from the beginning about how you died. Then I could have at least told Andy to dig elsewhere. And I'd have been prepared to deal with Maria and her bohunk husband. I don't know why they are so strung out about people finding out they're a couple of murderers, but they are very intent on keeping what happened to you a big old myst—"

"That," Jesse said, "is because to them, no time has passed since their deaths. They were at rest until it became evident that my body was about to be found, which would inevitably open up speculation as to the cause of my demise. They do not understand that more than a century has passed since then. They are trying to preserve their places in the community, as the leading citizens they once were."

"Tell me about it," I said, fingering my bruise. "They think it's still 1850, and they're afraid of the neighbors finding out they offed you. Well, it's all going to blow up in their faces in a day or so. The truth is coming out, courtesy of the *Carmel Pine Cone*—"

Jesse spun me around to face him. He looked madder than ever. "Susannah," he said. "What

276

are you talking about?"

"I told the whole story to CeeCee," I explained, unable to keep a note of self-congratulation from creeping into my voice. "She's interning at the paper for the summer. She says they're running the story—the real story, about what happened to you—on Sunday."

Seeing his expression growing, if anything, even darker, I added, "Jesse, I had to. Maria killed the guy at the historical society—the one she stole your picture from in order to do the exorcism. I'm pretty sure she killed his grandfather, too. Maria and that husband of hers have killed everybody who has ever tried to tell the truth about what really happened to you that night. But she's not going to be able to do it anymore. That story is going to go out to thirty-five thousand people. More even, because they'll post it on the paper's website. Maria isn't going to be able to kill everybody who reads it."

Jesse shook his head. "No, Susannah. She'll just settle for killing you."

"Jesse," I said. "She can't kill me. She's already tried. I've got news for you: I am really, really hard to kill."

"Maybe not," Jesse said. He held something out in his hand. I looked down at it. To my surprise, I saw that it was the rope we'd been following.

Only instead of the end disappearing down into the hole through which I'd climbed, it sat, frayed, in Jesse's hand. As if it had been cut.

Cut with a knife.

chapter *sixteen*

I stared down at the end of the rope in horror.

It's funny. You know what the first thing that popped into my head was?

"But Father Dom said," I cried, "that Maria and Felix were good Catholics. So what are they doing down in that church?"

Jesse had a little more presence of mind than I did. He reached out and seized my wrist, twisting it so he could see the face of Father Dominic's watch.

"How much more time do you have?" he demanded. "How many more minutes?"

I swallowed. "Eight," I said. "But the whole reason Father Dom blessed my house was so they wouldn't try to come in, and then look what they do. They come into a church—"

Jesse looked around. "We'll find the way out," he said. "Don't worry, Susannah. It has to be around here somewhere. We'll find it."

But we wouldn't. I knew that. There was no point, I knew, even in looking. What with the fog covering the ground so thickly, there was no chance we'd ever find the hole through which I'd climbed.

No. Susannah Simon, who'd been so hard to kill, was effectively dead already.

I started untying the rope from around my waist. If I was going to meet my maker, I at least wanted to look my best.

"It must be here," Jesse was saying as he waved at the fog, trying to part it in order to see beneath it. "Susannah, it must be."

I thought about Father Dominic. And Jack. Poor Jack. If that rope had been cut, it could only have been because something catastrophic had happened down in the church. Maria de Silva, that practicing Catholic Father D. had been so convinced would never dare launch an attack on consecrated ground, had not been as frightened of offending the Lord as Father Dominic had assumed she'd be. I hoped he and

Jack were all right. Her problem was with me, not them.

"Susannah." Jesse was peering down at me. "Susannah, why aren't you looking? You cannot give up, Susannah. We'll find it. I know we'll find it."

I just looked at him. I wasn't even seeing him, really. I was thinking about my mother. How was Father Dominic going to explain it? I mean, if he wasn't already dead himself. My mom was going to be really, really suspicious if my body was found in the basilica. I mean, I wouldn't even go to church on Sunday. Why would I be there on a Friday night?

"Susannah!" Jesse had reached out and seized me by both my shoulders. Now he gave me a shake with enough force to send my hair flying into my face. "Susannah, are you listening to me? We only have five more minutes. We've got to find a way out. Call him."

I blinked up at him, confusedly pushing my long dark hair from my eyes. That was one thing, anyway. I'd never have to worry about finding the perfect shade to cover my gray. I'd never turn gray now.

"Call who?" I asked dazedly.

"*The gatekeeper*," Jesse said through gritted

teeth. "You said he was your friend. Maybe he'll show us the way."

I looked into Jesse's eyes. I saw something in them I'd never seen before. I realized, in a rush, what that something was.

Fear. Jesse was afraid.

And suddenly I was afraid, too. Before I'd just been shocked. Now I was scared. Because if Jesse was afraid, well, that meant something really, really bad was about to happen. Because Jesse does not scare easily.

"Call him," Jesse said again.

I tore my gaze from his and looked around. Everywhere—everywhere I looked—I saw only fog, night sky, and more fog. No gatekeeper. No hole back to the Junipero Serra Mission church. No hallway filled with doors. Nothing.

And then, suddenly, there was something. A figure, striding toward us. I was filled with relief. The gatekeeper, at last. He would help me. I knew he would. . . .

Except that, as he came closer, I saw it wasn't the gatekeeper at all. This guy didn't have anything on his head except hair. Curly brown hair. Just like—

"Paul?" I burst out incredulously.

I couldn't believe it. Paul. Paul Slater. Paul

Slater was coming toward us. But how—

"Suze," he said conversationally as he strolled up. His hands were in the pockets of his chinos, and his Brooks Brothers shirt was untucked. He looked as if he had just breezed in from a long day on the golf course.

Paul Slater. *Paul Slater*.

"What are you doing here?" I asked. "Are you . . . are you dead?"

"I was about to ask you the same question," Paul said. He looked at Jesse, who was still clutching my shoulders. "Who's your friend? He is a friend, I assume."

"I—" I glanced from Jesse to Paul and then back again. "I came up here to get him," I explained. "He's my friend. My friend Jesse. Jack accidentally exorcised him, and—"

"Ah," Paul said, rolling back and forth on his heels. "Yes. I told you that you should have left well enough alone with Jack. He'll never be one of us, you know."

I just stared at him. I could not figure out what was happening. Paul Slater, here? It didn't make any sense. Not unless he was dead. "One of . . . what?"

"One of us," Paul repeated. "I told you, Suze. All this do-gooding, mediator nonsense. I can't believe you fell for it." He shook his head, chuckling a little. "I would have thought you were smarter than that. I mean, the old man, I can understand. He's from a completely different world—a different generation. And Jack, of course, is . . . well, clearly unsuited for this sort of thing. But you, Suze. I'd have expected more from you."

Jesse let go of my shoulders but kept one hand firmly around one of my wrists . . . the wrist with Father Dominic's watch on it. "This," he said, "is not the gatekeeper, I take it."

"No," I said. "This is Jack's brother, Paul. Paul?" I looked at him. "How did you get here? Are you dead?"

Paul rolled his eyes. "No. Please. And you didn't need to go through all that rigmarole to get here, either. You can, like me, come and go from here when you please, Suze. You've just been spending so much time 'helping'"—he made quotation marks in the air with his fingers—"lost souls like that one"—he nodded his head in Jesse's direction—"you've never had a chance to concentrate on discovering your real potential."

I stared at him. "You told me . . . you told me you don't believe in ghosts."

He smiled like a kid with his hand caught in

the cookie jar. "I should have been more specific," he said. "I don't believe in letting them walk all over me, like you clearly seem to." His gaze roved over Jesse contemptuously.

I was still having trouble processing what I was seeing . . . and hearing.

"But . . . but isn't that what mediators are supposed to do?" I stammered. "Help lost souls?"

Paul heaved a shudder, as if the fog swirling around us had suddenly grown colder. "Hardly," he said. "Well, maybe the old man. And the boy. But not me. And certainly not you, Susannah. And if you'd bothered giving me the time of day, instead of being so caught up trying to rescue this one."—he sneered in Jesse's direction—"I might have been able to show you precisely what you're capable of. Which is so much more than you can begin to imagine."

A glance at Jesse told me that I had better cut this little conversation short if I didn't want any bloodshed. I could see a muscle I'd never noticed before leaping in Jesse's jaw.

"Paul," I said. "I want you to know that it really means a lot to me, the fact that you, apparently, have your finger on the pulse of the mystical world. But right now, if I don't get back to earth, I'm going to wake up dead. Not to mention the fact that if I'm not mistaken, your little brother might be having a really hard time down there with a guy named Diego and a chick in a hoop-skirt."

Paul nodded. "Yes," he said. "Thanks to you and your refusal to acknowledge your true calling, Jack's life is in danger, as is, incidentally, the priest's."

Jesse made a sudden motion toward Paul, which I cut short by holding up a restraining hand.

"How about giving us some help then, huh, Paul, if you know so much?" I asked. It was no joke, holding Jesse back. He seemed ready to tear the guy's head off. "How do we get out of here?"

Paul shrugged. "Oh, is that all you want to know?" he asked. "That's easy. Just go into the light."

"Go into the—" I broke off, furious. *"Paul!"*

He chuckled. "Sorry," he said. "I just wanted to know if you'd seen the movie."

But he wasn't chuckling a bit a split second later when Jesse suddenly launched himself at him.

I'm serious. It was way WWF. One minute Paul

was standing there, smirking, and the next, Jesse's fist was sinking into his tanned, handsome face.

Well, I'd tried to stop him. Paul was, after all, probably my only way out of there. But I can't say I really minded when I heard the sound of nasal cartilage tearing.

Paul was pretty much a baby about the whole thing. He started cursing and saying stuff like, "You broke my nose! I can't believe you broke my nose!"

"I'll break more than your nose," Jesse declared, clutching Paul by his shirt collar and waving his blood-smeared fist in front of his eyes, "if you don't tell us how to get out of here *now*."

How Paul might have responded to this interesting threat I never did find out. That's because I heard a sweetly familiar voice call my name. I turned around, and there, running toward me through the mist, was Jack.

Around his waist was a rope.

"Suze," he called. "Come quick! That mean lady ghost you warned me about, she cut your rope, and now she and that other one are beating up Father Dominic!" Then he stopped running, took in the sight of Jesse still clutching a bloody-faced Paul, and said, curiously, "Paul? What are *you* doing here?"

A moment passed. A heartbeat, really—if I'd had one, which, of course, I didn't. No one moved. No one breathed. No one blinked.

Then Paul looked up at Jesse and said, "You'll regret this. Do you understand? I'll make you sorry."

Jesse just laughed, without the slightest trace of humor, and said, "You're welcome to try."

Then he tossed Paul aside as if he were a used tissue, strode forward, seized my wrist, and dragged me toward Jack.

"Take us to them," he said to the little boy.

And Jack, slipping his hand into mine, did so, without looking back at his brother. Not even once.

Which told me, I realized, just about everything—except what I really wanted to know:

Just who—or, more aptly, *what*—was Paul Slater?

But I didn't have time to stay and find out. Father Dominic's watch gave me a minute to return to my body, or be placed in the difficult position of not having one . . . which was going to make starting the eleventh grade in the fall a real problem.

Fortunately, the hole was not far from where we'd been standing. When we got to it and I looked down, I couldn't see Father Dominic anywhere. I could hear the sounds of a struggle, though—breaking glass, heavy objects hitting the floor, wood splintering.

And I could see my body, stretched out beneath me as if I were sleeping, and sleeping so deeply I wasn't stirring at the sound of all that racket. Not a twitch.

Somehow, it seemed a much longer way down than it had climbing up.

I turned to look at Jack. "You should go first," I said. "We'll lower you with the rope—"

But both he and Jesse shouted, "No!" at the same time.

And the next thing I knew, I was falling. Really. Down and down I tumbled, and while I couldn't see much as I fell, I could see what I was about to land on, and let me tell you, I did not relish crushing my own . . .

But I didn't. Just like in dreams I've had where I've been falling, I opened my eyes at the moment of impact, and found myself blinking up at Jesse's and Jack's faces, peering down at me over the rim of the hole Father Dom had created with his chanting.

I was inside myself again. And I was in one piece. I could tell as I reached down to make sure my legs were still there. They were. Everything was functional. Even the bruise on my head hurt again.

And when, a second later, a statue of the Virgin Mary—the one Adam had told me had wept blood—landed across my stomach, well, that really hurt, too.

"There she is," Maria de Silva cried. "Get her!"

I have to tell you, I am getting really tired of people—particularly dead people—trying to kill me. Paul is right: I *am* a do-gooder. I do nothing but try to help people, and what do I get for my efforts? Virgin Mary statues in the midriff. It isn't fair.

To show just how unfair I thought it all was, I heaved the statue off me, scrambled to my feet, and grabbed Maria by the back of her skirt. Apparently, recalling her last incident with me, she decided to make a run for it. Too late, though.

"You know, Maria," I said conversationally as I reeled her in by her flounces, the way a fisherman reels in a really big trout. "Girls like you really irritate me. I mean, it's not just that you get guys to do your dirty work for you, instead of doing it yourself. It's this whole I'm-so-much-better-than-you-because-I'm-a-de-Silva thing that really bugs me. Because this is America." I reached out and grabbed a fistful of her glossy black curls. "And in America, we're all created equal, whether our last name is de Silva or Simon."

"Yes?" Maria cried, lashing out with her knife. She'd apparently gotten it back. "Well, do you want to know what irritates me about you? You think that just because you are a mediator, you are better than me."

I have to tell you, that one cracked me up.

"Now that's not true," I said, ducking as she took a swipe at me with her blade. "I don't think I'm better than you because I'm a mediator, Maria. I think I'm better than you because I do not go around agreeing to marry guys I'm not in love with."

In a flash, I had her arm pinned behind her waist again. The knife fell to the floor with a clatter. "And even if I did," I went on, "I wouldn't have them murdered just so I could marry somebody else. Because"—keeping a firm grip on her hair with my other hand, I steered her toward the altar rail—"I believe the key to a successful relationship is communication. If you had simply communicated with Jesse better, none of this would be happening now. I mean, that's your real problem right there, Maria. Communication goes two ways. Somebody has to talk. And somebody has to listen."

Seeing what I was about to do, Maria shrieked, "Diego!"

But it was too late. I had already rammed her face, hard, into the altar rail.

"The thing is," I explained as I pulled her head back from the rail to examine the extent of the damage, "you won't listen, either, will you? I mean, I told you not to mess with me. And"—I leaned forward to whisper in her ear—"I think I specified that you not mess with my boyfriend, either. But did you listen? No . . . you . . . did . . . not."

I accompanied each of those last four words with a blow to Maria's face. Cruel, I know, but let's face it: She totally deserved it. The bitch had tried to kill me, not once, but twice.

Not that I'm counting or anything.

Here's the thing about chicks who were brought up in the nineteenth century: They're sneaky. I'll give them that. They have the whole back-stabbing, attacking-people-while-they're-asleep thing down pretty pat.

But as far as actual hand-to-hand combat

goes? Yeah, not so good at that. I broke her neck pretty easily just by stomping on it. In Prada slides, too!

It was a shame her neck wouldn't stay broken for long.

But while I had her nicely subdued, I looked around to see if Jack had made it down okay. . . .

And the news was not good. Oh, Jack was fine. It was just that he was hunched over Father Dominic, who was far from it. He was lying in a crumpled heap to one side of the altar, looking way worse for wear. I climbed over the altar rail and went to him.

"Oh, Suze," Jack wailed. "I can't wake him up! I think he's—"

But even as he was speaking, Father Dom, his bifocals askew on his face, let out a moan.

"Father D.?" I lifted his head and set it down gently in my lap. "Father D., it's me, Suze. Can you hear me?"

Father D. just moaned some more. But his eyelids fluttered, which I knew was a good sign.

"Jack," I said. "Run over there to that gold box beneath the crucifix—see it?—and pull out the decanter of wine you'll find there."

Jack hurried to do as I had asked. I put my face

close to Father Dominic's and whispered, "You'll be okay. Hang on, Father D. Keep it together."

A very loud, splintering crash distracted me, and I glanced around the rest of the church with a sudden sinking feeling. Diego. He was here somewhere. I'd forgotten all about him—

But Jesse hadn't.

I don't know why, but I had simply assumed that Jesse had stayed up there in that creepy shadowland. He hadn't. He had slipped back into this world—the real world—without, apparently, much thought as to what he might be giving up in doing so.

On the other hand, down here he was getting to beat the crap out of the guy who killed him, so maybe he wasn't giving up all that much. In fact, he looked pretty intent on returning the favor— you know, killing the guy who'd killed him— except, of course, that he couldn't, since Diego was already dead.

Still, I had never seen anybody go after someone with such single-minded purpose. Jesse, I was convinced, wasn't going to be satisfied merely with breaking Felix Diego's neck. No, I think he wanted to rip out the guy's spine.

And he was doing a pretty good job of it, too.

Diego was bigger than Jesse, but he was also older, and not as quick on his feet. Plus, I think Jesse just plain wanted it more. To see his opponent decapitated, I mean. At least, if the energy with which he was swinging a jagged-edged piece of pew at Felix Diego's head was any indication.

"Here," Jack said breathlessly as he brought the wine, in its crystal decanter, to me.

"Good," I said. It wasn't whiskey—isn't that what you're supposed to give unconscious people to rouse them?—but it had alcohol in it. "Father D.," I said, raising his head and putting the unstoppered decanter to his lips. "Drink some of this."

Only it didn't work. Wine just dribbled down his chin and dripped onto his chest.

Meanwhile, Maria had begun to moan. Her broken neck was snapping back into place already. That's the thing about ghosts. They bounce back, and way too fast.

Jack glared at her as she tried to raise herself to her knees.

"Too bad we can't exorcise *her*," he said darkly.

I looked at him. "Why can't we?" I asked.

Jack raised his eyebrows. "I don't know. We don't have the chicken blood anymore."

"We don't need the chicken blood," I said. "We have that." I nodded toward the circle of candles. Miraculously, in spite of all the fighting going on, they had remained standing.

"But we don't have a picture of her," Jack said. "Don't we need a picture of her?"

"Not," I said, gently putting Father D.s head back on the floor, "if we don't have to summon her. And we don't. She's right here. Come on and help me move her."

Jack took her feet. I took her torso. She moaned and fought us the whole way, but when we laid her on the choir robes, she must have felt as I did—that it was pretty darn comfortable— since she stopped struggling and just lay there. Above her head, the circle Father Dom had opened remained open, smoke—or fog, as I knew it was now—curling down from its outer edges in misty tendrils.

"How do we make it suck her in?" Jack wanted to know.

"I don't know." I glanced at Jesse and Diego. They were still engaged in what appeared to be mortal combat. If I had thought Jesse had lost the upper hand, I'd have gone over and helped, but it appeared he was doing fine.

Besides, the guy had killed him. I figured it was

payback time, and for that, Jesse did not need my help.

"The book!" I said, brightening. "Father Dom read from a book. Look around. Do you see it?"

Jack found the small, black, leather-bound volume beneath the first pew. When he flipped through the pages, however, his face fell.

"Suze," he said. "It's not even in English."

"That's okay," I said, and I took it from him and turned to the page Father Dominic had marked. "Here it is."

And I began to read.

I'm not going to pretend I know Latin. I don't. I hadn't the slightest idea what I was saying.

But I guess pronunciation doesn't count when you are summoning the forces of darkness, since, as I spoke, those misty tendrils began to grow longer and longer, until finally they spilled out onto the floor and began to curl around Maria's limbs.

She didn't even seem to mind, either. It was like she was enjoying the way they felt around her wrists and ankles.

Well, the chick was kind of dominatrixy, if you asked me.

She didn't even struggle when, as I read further, the slack on the smoky tendrils tightened, and slowly, the fog began elevating her off the floor.

"Hey," Jack said in an indignant voice. "How come it didn't do that for you? How come you had to climb into the hole?"

I was afraid to reply, however. Who knew what would happen if I stopped reading?

So I kept on. And Maria soared higher and higher, until . . .

With a strangled cry, Diego broke away from Jesse and came racing toward us.

"You bitch!" he bellowed at me as he stared in horror at his wife's body, dangling in the air above us. "Bring her down!"

Jesse, panting, his shirt torn down the middle and a thin ribbon of blood running down the side of his face from a cut in his forehead, came up behind Diego and said, "You want your wife so badly, then why don't you go to her?"

And he shoved Felix Diego into the center of the ring of candles.

A second later, tendrils of smoke shot down to curl around him, too.

Diego didn't take his exorcism as quietly as his wife. He did not appear to be enjoying himself one bit. He kicked and screamed and said quite a lot of stuff in Spanish that I didn't understand, but which Jesse surely did.

Still, Jesse's expression did not change, not even once. Every so often I looked up from what I was reading and checked. He watched the two lovers—the one who had killed him and the one who had ordered his death—disappear into the same hole we'd just climbed down from.

Until finally, after I'd uttered a last "Amen," they disappeared.

When the last echo of Diego's vengeful cries died away, silence filled the church. It was so pervasive a silence, it was actually a little overwhelming. I myself was reluctant to break it. But I felt like I had to.

"Jesse," I said softly.

But not softly enough. My whisper, in the stillness of the church, after all that violence, sounded like a scream.

Jesse tore his gaze from the hole through which Maria and Diego had disappeared and looked at me questioningly.

I nodded toward the hole. "If you want to go back," I said, though each word tasted, I was sure, like those beetles Dopey had accidentally poured into his mouth, "now is the time, before it closes up again."

Jesse looked up at the hole, and then at me,

and then back at the hole.

And then back at me.

"No, thank you, *querida*," he said casually. "I think I want to stay and see how it all ends."

chapter *seventeen*

How it all ended that day was with Jack and Jesse and me helping Father Dominic, when he finally came around, to a phone, so that he could call the police and report that he'd stumbled across a pair of thieves looting the place.

A lie, yes. But how else was he going to explain all the damage Maria and Diego had done? Not to mention the bump on his noggin.

Then, once we were sure the police and an ambulance were on their way, Jesse and I left Father Dominic and waited with Jack for the cab we'd called, carefully not talking about the one thing I'm pretty sure we were all thinking: Paul.

Not that I didn't try to get Jack to tell me what

was up with his brother and all. Basically, the conversation went like this:

Me: "So, Jack. What is up with your brother?"

Jack: (scowling) "I don't want to talk about it."

Me: "I can fully appreciate that. However, he appears to be able to move freely between the realms of the living and the dead, and I find this alarming. Do you think it is possible that he is the son of Satan?"

Jesse: "Susannah."

Me: "I mean that in the nicest possible way."

Jack: "I said I don't want to talk about it."

Me: "Which is perfectly understandable. But did you know before now that Paul is a mediator, too? Or were you as surprised as we were? Because you didn't seem very surprised when you ran into him, you know, up there."

Jack: "I really don't want to talk about this right now."

Jesse: "He doesn't want to talk about it, Susannah. Leave the boy alone."

Which was easy for Jesse to say. Jesse didn't know what I did. Which was that Paul and Maria and Diego . . . they had all been in cahoots. It had taken me a while to realize it, but now that I had, I could have kicked myself for not seeing it before: Paul's keeping me occupied at Friday's while Maria had Jack perform the exorcism on Jesse. Paul's remark—"It's easier to catch flies with honey than with vinegar." Hadn't Maria said the exact same thing to me, not a few hours later?

The three of them—Paul, Maria, and Diego—had formed an unholy trinity, bound, apparently by a common hatred of one person: Jesse.

But what possible reason could Paul, who'd never even met Jesse until that moment in purgatory, have to hate him? Now, of course, his dislike was understandable: Jesse had done him a very great bodily injury, something for which Paul had sworn to repay him next time he saw him. I'm sure Jesse wasn't taking it too seriously, but I was worried. I mean, I'd just gone to a lot of trouble to get Jesse out of one sticky situation. I wasn't too enthused about seeing him plunge straight into another one.

But it was no good. Jack wouldn't talk. The kid was traumatized. Well, sort of. He actually seemed like he'd had a pretty good time. He just didn't want to talk about his brother.

Which bummed me out. Because I had a lot of questions. For instance, if Paul was a mediator—and he had to be; how else could he have been walking around up there?—why hadn't he helped his little brother out with the whole I-see-dead-people thing, said a few words of encouragement, assured the poor kid he wasn't crazy?

But if I'd hoped to get any answers out of Jack on that account, I was sadly disappointed.

I guess if I'd had a brother like Paul, I probably wouldn't have wanted to talk about it either.

Once Jack had been safely dropped off at the hotel, Jesse and I began the long walk home (I didn't have enough money on me for a ride from the hotel back to my house).

You might wonder what we talked about during that two-mile trek. A lot, surely, might have been discussed.

And yet, to tell you the truth, I can't remember. I don't think we really talked about anything important. What was there to say, really?

I snuck in as successfully as I'd snuck out. No one woke up, except the dog, and once he saw it was me, he went right back to sleep. No one had noticed that I'd been gone.

No one ever does.

Spike was the only one besides me who'd noticed Jesse was gone, and his joy at seeing him again was an embarrassment to felines everywhere. I could hear the stupid cat purring all the way across the room. . . .

Although I didn't listen for long. That's because what happened was, I walked in, pulled down the bedclothes, slipped off my slides, and climbed into bed. I didn't even wash my face. I climbed into bed, looked one last time at Jesse as if to reassure myself he was really back, and then I went to sleep.

And I stayed asleep until Sunday.

My mother became convinced I was coming down with mono. At least until she saw the bruise on my forehead. Then she decided I was suffering from an aneurysm. Much as I tried to convince her that neither of these things was true—that I was just really, really tired—she didn't believe me, and would, I'm convinced, have dragged me to the hospital Sunday morning for an MRI—hey, I had been asleep for almost two days—except that she and Andy had to drive up to Doc's camp to bring him home.

The thing is, I guess dying—even for just half an hour—can be very exhausting.

I woke ravenous with hunger. After my mom and Andy left—having extracted from me a promise that I would not leave the house all day, but would instead wait meekly for them to return, so that they could reassess my state of health at that time—I downed two bagels and a bowl of Special K before Sleepy and Dopey even showed up at the table, looking all tousle-headed and unkempt. I, on the other hand, had already showered and dressed, and was ready to face the day . . . or at least unemployment, since I wasn't certain the Pebble Beach Hotel and Golf Resort was going to extend my contract with them, due to my having missed two days of work in a row.

Sleepy, however, reassured me on that account.

"Naw, it's cool," he said as he shoveled Cheerios into his mouth. "I talked to Caitlin. I told her you were going through, you know, a thing. On account of the dead dude in the backyard. She was okay with it."

"Really?" I wasn't actually listening to Sleepy. Instead, I was watching Dopey eat, always an awe-inspiring sight. He stuffed one entire half of a bagel into his mouth and seemed to swallow it whole. I wished I had a camera so I could record the event for posterity. Or at least prove to the next girl who declared my stepbrother a babe how wrong she was. I watched as, without lifting his gaze from the newspaper spread out before him, Dopey stuffed the other half of the bagel into his mouth and, again without chewing, ingested it, the way snakes devour rats.

It was the most disgusting thing I'd ever seen. Well, apart from the beetles in the orange juice container.

"Oh." Sleepy leaned back in his chair and plucked something from the counter behind him. "And Caitlin said to give this to you. It's from the Slaters. They checked out yesterday."

I caught the envelope he tossed. It was lumpy. There was something hard in it. SUSAN, it said, on the outside.

"They weren't supposed to check out until today," I said, ripping the envelope apart.

"Well." Sleepy shrugged. "They left early. What can I tell you?"

I read the first letter enclosed in the envelope. It was from Mrs. Slater. It said,

> *Dear Susan,*
> *What can I say? You did such*
> *wonders for our Jack. He is like a*
> *different boy. Things have always been*
> *much harder for Jack than for Paul.*
> *Jack just isn't as bright as Paul, I*
> *suppose. In any case, we were very*
> *sorry not to be able to say good-bye,*
> *but we did have to leave earlier than*
> *expected. Please accept this small*

*token of our appreciation, and know
that Rick and I are eternally in
your debt.*

Nancy Slater

Folded into this note was a check for two hundred dollars.

I'm not kidding. That wasn't my pay for the week, either. That was my *tip*.

I laid the check and the letter down beside my cereal bowl and took the next note out of the envelope. It was from Jack.

*Dear Suze,
You saved my life. I know you don't
believe it, but you did. If you hadn't
done what you did for me, I would
still be afraid. I don't think I will ever
be afraid again. Thank you, and I hope
your head feels better. Write to me if
you ever get a chance.*

Love, Jack

*P.S. Please don't ask me any more
about Paul. I'm sorry about what he
did. I'm sure he didn't mean it. He is
not so bad. J*

Oh, right, I thought cynically. *Not so bad?* The guy was a creep! He could walk freely within the land of the dead, and yet when his own brother was being terrified out of his wits by the fact that he could see dead people, the guy didn't lift a finger to explain. Not so bad. The guy was *very* bad. I sincerely hoped I never saw him again.

There was a second postscript to Jack's letter.

> *P.P.S. I thought you might want to have this. I don't know what else to do with it. J*

I tilted the envelope, and to my great surprise, out popped the miniature of Jesse I'd seen on Clive Clemmings's desk, back at the historical society. I looked down at it, stunned.

I would have to give it back. That was my first thought. I had to give it back. I mean, wouldn't I? You can't just keep things like that. That would be like stealing.

Except that somehow, I didn't think Clive would mind. Especially after Dopey looked up from the paper and went, "Yo, we're in here."

Sleepy glanced up from the automobile section he'd been scanning, as usual, for a '67 black Camaro with less than 50,000 miles.

"Get out," he said in a bored voice.

"No, seriously," Dopey said. "Look."

He turned the paper around, and there was a picture of our house. Alongside it was a photo of Clive Clemmings and a reproduction of Maria's portrait.

I snatched the paper away from Dopey.

"Hey," he yelled. "I was reading that!"

"Let somebody who can pronounce all the big words have a try," I said.

And then I read CeeCee's article out loud for both of them.

She'd written, basically, the same story I'd told her, starting with the discovery of Jesse's body—only she called him Hector, not Jesse, de Silva—and then going into Clive's grandfather's theory about his murder. She hit all the right points, hammering it home about Maria's two-faced treachery and Diego's overall ickiness. And without coming out and saying so in as many words, she managed to indicate that none of the couple's offspring ever amounted to much of anything.

Rock on, CeeCee.

She credited all of her information to the late Dr. Clive Clemmings, Ph.D., who she claimed had been piecing together the mystery at the time of his death a few days earlier. I had a feeling that

Clive, wherever he was, was going to be pleased. Not only did he come off looking like a hero for having solved a 150-year-old murder mystery, but they'd also managed to find a photo of him in which he still had most of his hair.

"Hey," Dopey said when I was finished reading. "How come they never mentioned me? I'm the one who found the skeleton."

"Oh, yeah," Sleepy said in disgust. "Your role was really crucial. After all, if it wasn't for you, the guy's skull might still be intact."

Dopey launched himself at his older brother. As the two of them rolled around on the floor, making a thunderous noise their father would never have put up with if he'd been home, I set the paper aside and returned to my envelope from the Slaters. There was still one more slip of paper inside it.

Suze, the strong, slanting handwriting on it read. *Apparently, it was not to be . . . for now.*

Paul. I couldn't believe it. The note was from Paul.

> *I know you have questions. I also know you have courage. What I wonder is whether you have the courage to ask the question that is*

*the hardest for someone of our . . .
persuasion.*

*In the meantime, remember: If
you give a man a fish, he'll eat for a
day. But if you teach him to fish, he'll
eat all the fish you might have caught
for yourself.*

*Just a little something to keep in
mind, Suze.*

Paul

Gosh, I thought. What a charmer. No wonder
we never clicked.

The hardest question of all? What was *that*? And
of what persuasion were we, precisely? What did
this guy know that I didn't? Plenty, apparently.

One thing I did know, though. Whatever else
Paul was—and I was not at all convinced he was
a mediator—he was a jerk. I mean Paul had pretty
much hung Jack out to dry not once, but twice,
first by never once bothering to say *Hey, don't
worry, kid, for folks like you and me, it's normal to
see dead people all over the place,* and the second
time by leaving him alone in that church while
those two psychos were tearing up the place.

Not to mention what, I was convinced, he'd
done to Jesse, someone he had not even known.

And for that, I'd never forgive him.

And I certainly wasn't about to trust him. Or his opinions on fishing.

Disgusted as I was with him, however, I didn't throw his note away. It would, I decided, have to be shown to Father Dom, who, a phone call had reassured me, was doing well—just a little sore, was all.

While Sleepy and Dopey rolled around—Dopey yelling, "Get offa me, homo"—I picked up my bounty and went back upstairs. Heck, it was my day off. I wasn't going to spend it indoors, despite my mother's orders. I decided to give CeeCee a call and see what she was up to. Maybe the two of us could hit the beach. I deserved, I thought, a little R and R.

When I got to my room, I saw that Jesse was already up. He doesn't usually pay morning visits. On the other hand, I don't normally sleep for thirty-six hours straight, so I guess neither of us was really sticking to the schedule.

In any case, I hadn't expected to see him there, and so I jumped about a foot and a half and quickly hid the hand carrying his miniature behind my back.

I mean, come on. I don't want him to think I *like* him or anything.

"You're awake," he said from the window seat where he'd been sitting with Spike and a copy of Abbie Hoffman's *Steal This Book* that I happen to know he'd stolen from my mother's bookshelf downstairs.

"Um," I said, sidling over to my bed. Maybe, if I was quick enough, I could thrust his picture under my pillow before he noticed. "Yes, I am."

"How do you feel?" he asked me.

"Me?" I asked, like there was somebody else in the room he could possibly have been asking.

Jesse laid the book down and looked at me with another one of those expressions on his face. You know, the kind I can never read.

"Yes, you," he said. "How do you feel?"

"Fine," I said. I made it to the bed. I sat down on it, and quick as a mongoose—I've never seen one in action, but I've heard they're pretty fast—I thrust the check, the letters, and the miniature under my pillow. Then I relaxed.

"I feel great," I said.

"Good," he said. "We need to talk."

Suddenly, I didn't feel so relaxed anymore. In fact, I sprang to my feet. I don't know why, but my heart started beating very fast.

Talk? What does he want to talk about? My mind was going a hundred miles a second. I suppose we should talk about what happened. I mean, it was very scary and all of that, and I nearly died, and like Paul said, I do have a lot of questions—

But what if that was what Jesse wanted to talk about? The part where I nearly died, I mean?

I didn't want to talk about that. Because the fact is, that whole part, that part where I nearly died, well, I nearly died trying to save *him*. Seriously. I was hoping he hadn't noticed, but I could tell by the look on his face that he totally had. Noticed, I mean.

And now he wanted to talk about it. But how could I talk about it? Without letting it slip? The L word, I mean.

"You know what," I said, very fast. "I don't want to talk. Is that okay? I really, really don't want to talk. I am all talked out."

Jesse lifted Spike off his lap and put him on the floor. Then he stood up.

What was he doing? I wondered. *What was he doing?*

I took a deep breath, and kept talking about not talking.

"I'm just—Look," I said, as he took a step toward me. "I'm just going to give CeeCee a call and maybe we'll go to the beach or something, because I really . . . I just need a day off."

Another step toward me. Now he was right in front of me.

"Especially," I said significantly, looking up at him, "from talking. That's what I especially need a day off from. *Talking*."

"Fine," he said. He reached up and cupped my face in both his hands. "We don't have to talk."

And that's when he kissed me.

On the lips.

Suze's supernatural misadventures
continue in the fifth Mediator book,

Haunted

The following is an excerpt:

He must have figured out from my expression
that all was not copacetic in Suze-and-Jesse-land,
since he laughed and said, "So that's how it is.
Well, I never really thought Jesse was your type,
you know. You need someone a little less—"

He didn't get a chance to finish his sentence,
because at that moment, CeeCee, who'd been
following Adam in the direction of his locker—
even though we'd solemnly sworn to each other
the night before over the phone that we were not
going to start off the new school year chasing
boys—came back toward us, her gaze on the guy
standing so close to me.

"Suze," she said politely. Unlike me, CeeCee
had spent her summer working in the non-profit
sector, and so had not had a lot of money to blow
on a back-to-school wardrobe and makeover.
Not that CeeCee would ever spend her money on

anything so frivolous as makeup. Which was a good thing, since, being an albino, she had to special-order all of her makeup anyway, and couldn't just stroll on up to the M.A.C. counter and plunk her money down the way anybody else could.

"Who's your friend?" she wanted to know.

I was not about to stand there and make introductions. In fact, I was seriously thinking of heading to the administrative office and asking just what they were thinking, admitting a guy like this into what I had once considered a passably good school.

But he thrust one of those cool, strong hands at CeeCee and said with that grin that I had once found disarming but that now chilled me to the bone, "Hi. I'm Paul. Paul Slater. Nice to meet you."

Paul Slater. Not really the kind of name to strike terror into the heart of a young girl, huh? I mean, it sounded innocuous enough. *Hi, I'm Paul Slater.* There was nothing in that statement that could have alerted CeeCee to the truth: Paul Slater was sick, manipulative, and had icicles where his heart should have been.

No, CeeCee had no clue. Because I hadn't told her, of course. I hadn't told anyone.

The more fool I.

If CeeCee found his fingers a little too cold for her liking, she didn't let on.

"CeeCee Webb," she said, as she pumped his hand in her typically businesslike manner. "You must be new here, because I've never seen you around before."

Paul blinked, bringing attention to his eye-lashes, which were really long, for a guy's. They looked almost heavy on his eyelids, like they'd be an effort to lift. My stepbrother Jake has sort of the same thing going, only on him, it just makes him look drowsy. On Paul, it had more of a sexy rock-star effect. I glanced worriedly at CeeCee. She was one of the most sensible people I had ever met, but are any of us really immune to the sexy rock-star type?

"My first day," Paul said with another one of those grins. "Lucky for me, I already happen to be acquainted with Ms. Simon here."

"How fortuitous," CeeCee, who, as editor of the school paper, liked big words, said, her white-blond eyebrows raised slightly. "Did you used to go to Suze's old school?"

"No," I said quickly. "He didn't. Look, we better get to homeroom, or we're going to get into trouble. . . ."

But Paul wasn't worried about getting into trouble. Probably because Paul was used to causing it.

"Suze and I had a thing this past summer," he informed CeeCee, whose purple eyes widened behind the lenses of her glasses at this information.

"A *thing*?" she echoed.

"There was no thing," I hastened to assure her. "Believe me. No thing at all."

CeeCee's eyes got even wider. It was clear she didn't believe me. Well, why should she? I was her best friend, it was true. But had I ever once been completely honest with her? No. And she clearly knew it.

"Oh, so you guys broke up?" she asked pointedly.

"No, we didn't break up," Paul said, with another one of those secretive, knowing smiles.

Because we were never going out, I wanted to shriek. You think I'd ever go out with *him*? He's not what you think, CeeCee. He *looks* human, but underneath that studly façade, he's a . . . a . . .

Well, I didn't know what Paul was, exactly.

But then, what did that make me? Paul and I had far more in common than I was comfortable admitting, even to myself.

Even if I'd had the guts to say something along

4

those lines in front of him, I didn't get a chance because suddenly a stern, "Miss Simon! Miss Webb! Haven't you ladies got a class you should be getting to?" rang out.

Sister Ernestine—whose three-month absence from my life had not rendered her any less intimidating, with her enormous chest and even bigger crucifix adorning it—came barreling down upon us, the wide black sleeves of her habit trailing behind her like wings.

"Get going," she tut-tutted us, waving her hands in the direction of our lockers, built into the adobe walls all along the mission's beautifully manicured inner courtyard. "You'll be late to first period."

We got going . . . but unfortunately Paul followed directly behind us.

"Suze and I go way back," he was saying to CeeCee, as we moved along the porticoed hallway toward my locker. "We met at the Pebble Beach Hotel and Golf Resort."

I could only stare at him as I fumbled with the combination to my locker. I couldn't believe this was happening. I really couldn't. What was Paul doing here? What was Paul doing here enrolling in my school, making my world—from which I'd thought I'd rid him forever—a real-life nightmare?

I didn't want to know. Whatever his motives for coming back, I didn't want to know. I just wanted to get away from him, get to class, anywhere, anywhere at all . . .

. . . so long as it was away from him.

"Well," I said, slamming my locker door closed. I hardly knew what I was doing. I had reached in and blindly grabbed the first books my fingers touched. "Gotta go. Homeroom calls."

He looked down at the books in my arms, the ones I was holding almost as a shield, as if they would protect me from whatever it was—and I was sure there was something—he had in store for me. For us.

"You won't find them in there," Paul said with a cryptic nod at the textbooks bulging from my arms.

I didn't know what he was talking about. I didn't *want* to know. All I knew was that I wanted out of there, and I wanted out of there fast. CeeCee still stood beside me, looking bewilderedly from my face to Paul's. Any second, I knew, she was going to begin to ask questions, questions I didn't dare answer . . . because she wouldn't believe me if I tried.

Still, even though I didn't want to, I heard myself asking, as if the words were being torn involuntarily from my lips, "I won't find what in here?"

"The answers you're looking for." Paul's blue-eyed gaze was intense. "Why you, of all people, were chosen. And what, exactly, you are."

This time, I didn't have to ask what he meant. I knew. I knew as surely as if he'd said the words out loud. He was talking about the gift we shared, he and I, the one over which he seemed to have so much better control—and of which he seemed to have such superior knowledge—than I did.

While CeeCee stood there, staring at the two of us as if we were speaking a foreign language, Paul went on smoothly, "When you're ready to hear the truth about what you are, you'll know where to find me. Because I'll be right here."

And then he walked away, seemingly unaware of all the feminine sighs he drew from my class-mates as he moved with pantherlike grace down the breezeway.

Her violet eyes still wide behind her glasses, CeeCee looked up at me wonderingly.

"What," she wanted to know, "was that guy talking about? And who on earth is *Jesse*?"

Read all the
Mediator books:

Meg Cabot is also the author of the Princess Diaries series, upon which the Disney movies are based. In the books, though, Princess Mia has yield-sign-shaped hair, lives in New York, and Fat Louie is orange. And those are the least of the differences. The following is a complete list of the Princess Diaries books:

THE PRINCESS DIARIES

THE PRINCESS DIARIES, VOLUME II:
PRINCESS IN THE SPOTLIGHT

THE PRINCESS DIARIES, VOLUME III:
PRINCESS IN LOVE

THE PRINCESS DIARIES, VOLUME IV:
PRINCESS IN WAITING

THE PRINCESS DIARIES, VOLUME IV AND A HALF:
PROJECT PRINCESS

THE PRINCESS DIARIES, VOLUME V:
PRINCESS IN PINK

THE PRINCESS DIARIES, VOLUME VI:
PRINCESS IN TRAINING

THE PRINCESS PRESENT:
A PRINCESS DIARIES BOOK

PRINCESS LESSONS:
A PRINCESS DIARIES BOOK

PERFECT PRINCESS:
A PRINCESS DIARIES BOOK

Aside from the Mediator books
and the Princess Diaries books, Meg
has written several more books:

ALL-AMERICAN GIRL

Samantha Madison saves the president's life...only to have his son fall in love with her. Which would be fine, except for all the Secret Service agents following them around.

teen IDOL

Jenny Greenley gives everyone advice, so why can't she follow her own and find love? Further complicating matters is the presence of hot Hollywood star Luke Striker in Jenny's home-room, of all places.

Nicola and the Viscount

It's 1810, and Nicola Sparks is ready to dive head-long into her first London Season. Good thing there's a handsome viscount there to catch her!

Victoria and the Rogue

Lady Victoria Arbuthnot is accustomed to being right. She isn't always, though, especially when her own heart is concerned.

But wait!
There's more by Meg:

THE BOY NEXT DOOR

BOY MEETS GIRL

EVERY BOY'S GOT ONE

THE 1-800-WHERE-R-YOU BOOKS:

WHEN LIGHTNING STRIKES

CODE NAME CASSANDRA

SAFE HOUSE

SANCTUARY

For more about Meg and
to read her diary, visit:

www.megcabot.com

Join her online book club at:

www.megcabotbookclub.com